BLACK GLOVES
WHITE MAGIC

BLACK GLOVES
WHITE MAGIC

A Collection of Stories From the
Editor of Vulcan American and Rubber Rebel Magazine

Tim Brough

Thanks for the support !

Tim Brough

A Boner Book by,
The Nazca Plains Corportion
Las Vegas, Nevada
2003

ISBN: 1-887895-50-7

Published by,

The Nazca Plains Corporation ®
4640 Paradise Rd, Suite 141
Las Vegas NV 89109-8000

PUBLISHER'S NOTE
This is a work of fiction. Names, characters, places, and incidents
either are the products of the author's imagination or are used ficti-
tiously, and any resemblance to actual persons, living or dead,
business establishments, events or locales is entirely coincidental.

Editor, Ty Evans

Photographer, Robert Bishop

Cover Model, Jayden

Cover Designer, Ty Evans

For Peter

Acknowledgements

I've often compared writing a short story to writing a pop song. Verse, verse, bridge, chorus, verse. Maybe it's just my deep-seated dream of being a Beatle or Elvis Costello, but there has always been some sort of music playing in my headphones while I write stories. Even the title of this book, was cribbed from a line in a song by the band Prefab Sprout. Some of the references are obvious (The title "Someday Never Comes"), some not (there is a reference to R.E.M. in "9 Tenths Of The Law" if you want to go looking). More than a few of these were written with Enigma, Steely Dan, or Costello CD's in the player. The Police and Todd Rundgren are in the background as I write this. I just have to have a sense of enigmatic occurrences and one of structure when I get down to the dirt. After all, the end result is I want you to reach down and stimulate yourself in the most intimate way one man can.

At the same time, I'd like to think I was doing more than writing disposable j/o ditties that would fade from memory faster than your cum rag was drying. That is why getting this volume into print is such an honor. There were enough requests for some of these old stories (in particular, the ones from Rubber Rebel), that I felt getting them into a single book would be worth the effort. It's a very satisfying thing to know that someone could come up to you, a total stranger, and say that they found a passage in a certain story so fucking hot that they had to try it themselves, or that someone found a copy of Rubber Rebel or Vulcan America and it helped them recognize what was inside their soul. I've always been frustrated by the endless parade of stories that seem to be connected by countless "And then He" connectors, like there was little else to discern the actions from a random grope in the dark. The characters I tired to put in each story were as far as random as I could make them, and I think on occasion I succeeded in making the stories heartfelt and horn-doggie at the same time.

Rubber Rebel was my intro to all this. I'd already had some success as a writer for business trade papers related to the broadcasting industry. Once a magazine I was working for in Nashville hit the dirt, I gathered my things and ran back to Los Angeles to rejoin my friends and join the ranks of the unemployed. When my friend photographer John Rand invited me to a Thanksgiving dinner at a friend's house in 1994, little did I know that it would be the start of what has culminated in the pages you hold before you. That was the day I met Peter Tolos, and he got me intrigued by a kinky magazine he had been producing for rubber enthusiasts. He perked up at the mention of my experience in layout and writing. By the end of the next month, I was working on what would become Rubber Rebel's fourth issue and my first sex story. We worked together on rubber publications till his passing in 1999, with Rubber Rebel and Vulcan America. And it has certainly been a long-strange-crazy-cool five years since I stood at the window of the North Hollywood Post Office and asked the clerk for enough postage to mail almost 300 magazines' worth of envelopes for Vulcan's first issue.

Between then and now, there has been all the usual living to be done. Nothing happens while you watch it, but eventually everything will happen. And does. And as anyone who has embarked on any kind of effort of this nature can tell you, it doesn't happen on its own. I wish I could thank everyone who has pitched in for Rubber Rebel, Vulcan America, and this book, but I'd probably have to start another book entitled "For Those Without Whom."

In alphabetical order:

Mikal Bales (Zeus Studios): You have encouraged me, given me advice, and held on to my hand in some of my darkest hours. Calling you "Daddy Zeus" is more than just an honorary.

Ron Borders and Hershey: Ronnie Bear, you waited for me for all those years. Then you kept my Hershey Dog! Thank you for three wonderful and tumultuous years, and for giving me everything you could.

Jack Fritscher (Palm Drive): I've said it before and I'll say it again, you make me a better writer. Thanks for never holding back.

Bert The Bear: From the final days of Rubber Rebel to the present day, you have been there. If not for you, the Vulcan America world would have never gone into (cyber) space. I will always have a special place in my heart for you and our days in Austin.

Dave Rhodes (The Leather Journal): Ever since I met you when I first got to Los Angeles, you've been there with support and friendship. You're the glue that keeps a lot of this fragile web work of Kink Kommunity in one piece.

Jack Rinella: You have the uncanny knack for taking the most complicated tangle of thoughts and emotions, then distilling them down to a few precisely accurate sentences. In 1994, you took a weekend out of my life that helped me understand what my future could be. Bless you and your family.

Robert Steele (Nazca Plains): You held on to these story files till the time was ripe.

And most importantly in the here and now, my Papa Joel, for making me feel breathless again.

A quick thanks to the following (in no particular order). MASTER GAINES, Master Steve Sampson, Master Darwin, Bob Reite, Gary "Skinner Jack" Taylor, Dave Kurn, James Bond, Roger Hickey and Dave Boyer of Chicago Cell Block, Marc Peurye, Jim Price, Young Master Bear, Papa Snake, MUT200, Raoul, Jimmy W., JFB, Joseph Bean, Chuck Renslow, Butch God, NYMaster, Ernie The Attorney, Andrew & Larry, Daddy Nick, Bill the Ropeman, Northwind, ROSS & ross, Thor, David S., slave matt, Dave Lavorn, Master Dennis, Papadoc, Mitch and Gerrie, Household Keppeler, Rob Cole, San Diego Dude, CALeather, Rich and David from the UK, Seniorkink and everyone else who will give me hell because I didn't list you.

Tim Brough

CONTENTS

BLACK GLOVES
WHITE MAGIC

THE COLOR OF COWARDS

He homed in on me just about as soon as I walked into the bar. Granted, coming to Los Angeles during Rodeo Weekend is a perilous exercise. There is still something of a division between bikers and cowboys, and the youngsters are just so uppity that you want to slap'em based on general principle. Not that it would've bothered me all that much. The whip I wear on my left hip ain't there just for affectation. I can rip a newspaper out of your hands just as easily as I can make a tissue bounce across the floor. So the leather I choose to wear isn't out of some South Of Market costume designer's backroom.

I worked an Oklahoma ranch for twenty-seven years. I've worn chaps against the sides of horses and motorcycles. I've cracked a lash at wayward cattle and insolent bottoms for more than a quarter century. When I chose to retire, it was to the high desert of eastern California, not to some resort town claiming it was a desert paradise. I bought a four-wheel drive pick-up because my house is five miles off the closest paved road, not because it looks butcher than thou.

I'm in shape because my idea of a good afternoon's recreation is dragging a bottom off on a hike along a mountain until I find a suitable place to throw down a camping tent, rope his ass tight and scare him with a fireside scene.

Now I come into town to help the IGRA as a volunteer. I decide to take time and hit some local watering holes before the very long drive home. Damn if the first thing I get is some snot nose city kid with attitude. Sitting right off the edge of the bar, all Mohawk, piercings, bike gear, and the Doc Martens...like they mean something. Without him even taking his jacket off, I knew that his arms were probably covered with a really crappy black-work tattoo. And I bet if anyone would get close enough to ask

3

him, he'd probably say he was one of the New Tribe. Whatever the fuck that is these days.

The kid looks at me, eyes lit with malicious glee, and snorts "Hey Pops, in case you hadn't noticed, this here's a leather bar."

I saunter up to the bar and order my usual: a shot of JD and a cold one. My best withering-but-world-weary glance is fired off in his direction, if he wasn't too drunk, he'd catch the sub text. Then again, he probably already was three sheets to the wind, or just plain old stupid, maybe both. Because he decided that he should let another zinger loose.

"Texas, old man? That's where everyone still wears that shit, right? Isn't that about 1500 miles east of here?"

I very deliberately take a cigar out from my vest and slide it out from the tube. With studied grace, I clip the end, strike a match against the patio brick of the bar and let the flame grow until it is long enough to give me the even light I need, and puff a few times until the cigar is burning to my satisfaction. I tilted the Stetson that my father gave to me at the age of eighteen back to make it plain that my blue eyes were still very focused above my long moustache... there since the only people who wore them were beatnicks, bikers, outlaws and ropers. Then another, darker stare at Mr. Mohawk and his cadre of pups, one that a boy with any etiquette would be able to translate as "Shut up now or face some real consequences."

Even though I noticed his pals were getting the message, Mr. Mohawk must've figured my silence meant he was holding a stronger hand. Even with his crew visibly backing off, he decided to lob another volley in my direction.

"Yeah, I used to want to be a cowboy when I was little. I wanted to be a fireman, too. Then I grew up."

I decided it was time to respond, but not without a bit of showmanship first. I signaled to the patio bartender, downed my shot of JD and flipped the glass like a shooter marble to the 'tender who caught it like a true pro. He refilled it and sat it back down on the counter in front of me. I downed that one just as effortlessly and took a swig of my beer. Then, picking up my cigar, I turned towards my young rival, leaned back against the bar and with my okie drawl attuned to the highest of ironic inflections, growled at this pious little shit "Unless I miss my guess, you moved to West Hollywood, started reading mags at Pleasure Chest and took a job as a 'telephone actor,' telling all your friends back home that you were still waiting for the right script to come along."

There must have been a grain of truth in there someplace, because his friends tittered more than a little. Mr. Mohawk also began showing a shade of red creeping up his malnourished neck. I continued along, "Then somewhere in some San Francisco sissy leather mag, discovered that cutting your hair real close and buying a nose ring along with a used leather jacket would make you a modern primitive. Using the money you had left over from getting closet cases to jack off for $3.99 a minute on the Visa Card, you went to some cheap needle butcher and got a big black ugly band of squares around your arm. Now you think that looking like some 1980 London fuck-up makes you a 1995 leather stud. So tell me punk," I asked, blowing a healthy stream of blue cigar haze over the bar, "how close to the bulls-eye am I? Your friends make me think I'm pretty damn close to the mark." I knew it, too. His eyes were wide enough to run a herd through and the red around his neck had managed a slow crawl to the fringes of his 'hawk.

"Fuck you, cowboy. How many sheep did you fuck in Texas?"

Even I had to laugh at that one. "For starts, boy, I'm from Oklahoma, so brush up on your geography. Second, I never had to worry about fucking the animals. By the time I was old enough to know I wanted to ride a saddle horse, I knew I wanted to fuck men. Before I even stuck a boot inside a men's bar, I made sure I understood the dichotomies of power and the dynamics of this lifestyle. Something you decided not to bother with, obviously."

"Old man knows some big words."

"Tell me boy, which word is most difficult for you 'Dichotomy', 'Geography', or perhaps 'Lifestyle'?"

Mr. Mohawk's little cluster of followers were looking at their leader a might bit anxiously. I figured that at least they got the message loud and clear, because they weren't sniggering any- more. With any luck, their body English would inform Mr. Mohawk that this old Cowboy was not to be trifled with. My body was already turning back to the bar counter, for my beer and cigar. But I guess the punk was too humiliated to know when to let go.

"The phony cowboy suit is tired, asshole. Get with the nineties. Brown leather is the color of cowards."

Up till now, I hadn't noticed that our exchange had been getting the attention of the patrons in the bar. I knew it then, though. The place went dead silent on the little whelp's comment, with all eyes and ears zeroing in on me wondering what my next move was going to be, and who was I to disappoint them? Besides, it was obviously time to give Mr. Mohawk a lesson in pro- priety. Although I hated to waste a good cigar, I crushed it under the heel of my boot, spun very slowly and pulled up to my full 5' 10", all rawhide vest, brown chaps, tan bullwhip, old style, sweat stained brown Stetson and desert-weathered moustache and face. If this crowd wanted a show and Mr. Mohawk wanted a confronta- tion, I decided to give them both the likes of which they would be talking about in hushed tones for a few years to come.

"Boy, I was wearin' brown leather before your parents shared their first milkshake and was ropin' cattle before you were watchin' Saturday morning cartoons. I roped my first boy and stuffed a gag in his mouth before you were even able to say your ABC's. I was smokin' cigars before you ate your first crayon. My hat has seen the dust of deserts and rodeos from the back of horses from Oklahoma to California and most of the lower forty- eight, even if you could name 'em, and Alaska, too.

"I've got some advice for you before I take you on a little trip. If you and your new wave friends decide to mess with out-of- towners again, you'd best start studying when the time to play

6

ends and the time to shut up starts, because I'm going to teach you a thing or two about the color of cowards..." a long pause for dramatic effect, "...and why the phrase 'meaner than dirt' didn't come from the color of black."

His face went pale as I moved, faster than white lightning, and pushed him over the edge of the bar. I had a coil of rope ready and had his hands neatly bound before he even made his first motion at getting out from under me. A couple of quick turns pinned his arms to his sides, and his ankles were soon up at his asshole. Why it took him this long to utter a protest i'll never know, but he finally started squirming and cussing. I'll take it as a measure of my support at the bar that the clerk of the leather shop popped a bridle-bit into the punk's mouth and fastened it into place for me. "Just thought a horsy gag was appropriate," was all he had to say.

A smattering of applause and cheers went up from the bar as I lifted my hog-tied little dogie off the counter and carted him out to my pick-up truck. I flipped his puppy-pals a business card and told them I'd be back with their friend on Tuesday. They could pick him up then, if they wanted anything to do with him. In the back of my truck, I ran a series of ropes around his armpits, knees and ankles to center him on some old cloth padding and I turned on a two way intercom between him and the main cab.

That way I could hear his grunts all the way to Wonder Valley and know that he was contemplating his near future. An old Chris LeDoux tape went into the cassette deck and we started the three hour drive to the nice, remote area where my ranch is located.

One hundred eighty miles gives anyone time to ponder. By the time I was pulling in from the dirt trail and into my compound, Mr. Mohawk had plenty of time to do some soul searching. I pulled him out from the bed of the truck, all sweat and fear-stink, and pulled the rubber horse gag from between his teeth. Blubbered words of "I'm sorry Sir" led me all the way to the fire pit and my Saint Andrews Cross that faced the rock wall of the mountains along the rear of my property. I undid the ropes around his Doc

Martens and let him shake some circulation back into his feet. Then I stood him up against the cross and pulled his feet apart, making him face the cliff wall. A couple of tedious but necessary maneuvers later, his back was bare and his arms were stretched over the upper portion of the cross. Just as I suspected; there was a twisty-curving network of black lines around his attempted bicep. I threw a couple of twigs and boards into the pit and there was a flickering after-dusk illumination of my new trophy. I listened "with delight as he moaned and struggled against the ropes, which had obviously frustrated his constant attempts to free himself during the trip here. He was still blubbering as I took another cigar, just like the first one at the bar, and lit it with a stick from the fire pit.

I took off my vest and stretched my muscular chest against his back, letting my hands roam along the indentations of his ribs. "The leather is gone," I whispered into his ear. "Who's acting like the coward now?"

More protests, more pleas. Mr. Mohawk was obviously frightened that he may have bitten off more than he could chew. "Don't worry, punk. Your friends got my name and number before we left. So don't worry about getting back to LA. They know who I am, and I'm not out to harm you. Just to teach you a thing or two about the leather and Cowboy lifestyle. This house was bought from over a quarter century of working the family cattle ranch. That's a lot of steak on your table, boy. I put the fence up around here ten years ago, there's security all around, the only way in is at the gate down the mountain. I don't think your pals are gonna try to follow you up here... they sure didn't do much to stop me from carting you out of the bar. I've got some things in the house that you're going to find very interesting, just wait here a minute." I bit his shoulder hard enough to leave some deep marks. He yelped, as I chuckled.

When I returned, it was with three new items. I took a deep draw on my cigar and moved to a place in front of the cross. "Take a good close look at these, boy," as I held up two of my favorites in front of him to view. "These will be the last two things you'll see before we start. They are identical six foot bullwhips. They were both made by the man who first taught me how to use them. He

8

didn't discriminate over colors. Look real, real close boy. See how long and snakelike they both are?" I pulled the tail of each under his nose. "Does either whip smell any different than the other? I'm gonna make a deal with you. I love whipping the tar out of stupid assholes like you. I can flick fleas off your scrawny little back or I could lay it wide open...I'm not sure which I really want to do. Or if I even want to waste time on your sorry flesh. So here is the twist, smart ass. I've got two bullwhips here. One is jet black. The other is the same brown you insulted in the bar this afternoon. If you're such a fucking authority on leather colors, you should have no trouble telling them apart, now will you?" I took the third item I brought out from the house and dangled it in front of his face. "Especially if you're wearing this." I took the blindfold and adjusted it over his head, pulling it down over his eyes and securing it...maybe just a touch rougher than necessary, but Mr. Mohawk was just reeking with the stink of fear, and it was getting me off.

"Even if you're not the hot-shit authority you claim to be, you still have a 50/50 chance of at least guessing correctly. Now...you were a very impolite, rude punk at the bar when I came in today. I didn't even get to finish my beer and had to throw out a cigar that I was barely halfway through. That's an even worse transgression than just your boorishness. So I figure that's worth at least ten lashes to start. But ten is barely enough to get my dick hard. I don't like doling out anything less than FIFTY"...SNAP!... "And a hundred is more my style" ...SNAP!... "Do you see where I'm heading, you stupid little pukeball?"

I was punctuating my talk with a good whip crack on either side of his head, and it had the desired effect. Mr. Mohawk jumped and shouted after each report, though the whip didn't even come within a foot of his ear.

"In case you don't, let me spell it out for you. Your going to get ten hits...five from each whip. If you can tell me, in the deep reaches of your refined wisdom, which color whip gave you the first or last five lashes, then I'll take you off the cross, lock you in the shed, and cart your useless ass back to LA tomorrow morning." He started really fighting with his ropes now. "If you're wrong, I'm going to have to fuck your ass through those macho black chaps of yours and give you another ninety strokes...with the brown whip, of course."

Mr. Mohawk was getting the picture. "Let me the hell down, man! I'm sorry about what I said! I was drunk, I didn't mean it, I'm sorry. Oh god, I'm sorry..." all the while thrashing like a fox in a trap. I liked it! He looked great in the firelight, all stretched out shoulders and sweaty spine. I just had to stand there for a second, enjoying my cigar and watching the motion. I felt it in my chaps, too. Even as a man of my word, his ass started beckoning.

I went around behind Mr. Mohawk and took a few silent warm up swings with the black bullwhip, judging the distance and my grip before landing the first blow. It landed with a heavy thud across his shoulders. I stepped up to his head, letting my skin press against his. "That's the first," I breathed into his ear. "Nine more. I hope you're paying close attention to how this feels, boy."

Back to my position behind my target and started striking off the rest of the four black whip strokes. Mr. Mohawk's cries echoed up the face of the mountain after each one. My dick was dripping pre-cum, but I had to temper myself. I approached my whipping boy. My dick pressed against his ass this time, my hands teased the welts.

"That's the first five, Picasso. The next five are with the second whip. Then I'll ask you your very important question. Brown then black? Or black then brown?"

Man, this was turning me on. I took a few quick warm-ups and then let fly with five successive brown whip blows across Mr. Mohawk's shoulders. Hearing his cries reminded me to hold back. I was sure that this pup had never felt the sting of a lash before tonight. These were virgin shoulders that I was raising marks upon.

After the fifth, he slumped against the cross. I approached him carefully, touching his shoulders like I would stroke fine China. "Listen close, asshole. Did I hit you with the black whip first, or the brown one? Only one hint," I cooed. "That brown whip is this

Cowboy's all time favorite. Got an answer for me, boy? Show me how smart you really are."

Moments later, his voice came out in a rasp. "Black then brown, Sir."

I hesitated. Lucky guess? Had to be. I wanted to fuck him so bad that I was contemplating lying and going for it anyhow. But that just isn't my style. I ran my fingers down his cheek and told him he was right.

"Thank you, Sir. Can I tell you how I knew?"

I paused. "Go ahead, boy."

"When you told me the brown whip was your favorite, it made it easier to guess, because the last five felt better than the first."

Well! Not as stupid as I first thought. That ass was still tempting.

"Sir, please, may I have more? With your brown whip, Sir?" Mr. Mohawk muttered from his position on the cross.

"You'll get them all, boy, and then some" I growled as I moved in behind him again and cracked the seal on a rubber. "But first this old Cowboy has a little something he has to take care of."

BAD SNEAKERS

My pants were undone, loose and open around my waist. I stood in the back yard, warm sun beating against the tool shed, away from where my nosy sisters could find me. Classmates had told me they'd "done it," and from their descriptions, it was so amazing that I had to find out if I could make it happen for me, too! Nervous hands and fingers, exploring just like the pictures in the magazines. My toes curled and crushed the padded cloth around my socks. That shivery feeling ran along my back. Then for the first time in my life, my boy cock did something that only a man's cock could do. I tossed my very first load. I let go of myself in shock, watching in awe as the magic fluid I'd only heard about in other guys' bragging stories came out of me, spurting down to the ground. It spattered on the grass, and all over my black canvas high tops.

That April afternoon changed my life forever. I recaptured the incident so many times that summer, that these two things have interlocked in my mind ever since. Sex equals sneakers. Within a few months, I realized I couldn't get myself off without the comfort of canvas and the warm smelly feel of rubber soles under my feet. Take those ingredients away, and it just didn't happen!

My sneaker love got me into plenty of trouble when I started going to bars where the other men were. Boots are hot, sure, but the other men didn't want to know about the guy with the basket-ball shoes on. I wasn't wearing the 'uniform' and was adamant about my fetish. Disillusionment started to settle in. If I couldn't get these hot men to share in my excitement, did that mean I was the only man who felt this way?

So I tried to become somebody else. I bought a set of boots just to wear in the bars. I compromised myself as little as possible, even my first pair of boots were rubber soled waders. At least they smelled like the sneakers I'd wished I was wearing. Instead of leather, though, I found myself being more and more attracted to rubber and vinyl gear. Some of the real hard-cores thought me a bit daft, but I couldn't get myself totally unhinged from my true feelings.

All this time, my sneaker collection continued to grow. I would climb into bed at night with a really funky pair of sneaks I'd found at a flea market, my face in one and my cock in the other. Breathing in the scent of asphalt, rubber and sweat, while humping away in the match! I broke in plenty of new pairs this way, too.

How I loved that gummy and gluey concentrated rush of smells fresh out of a brand new shoe box, when I'd tear away the tissue and lift a factory fresh sneaker to my nose and take it all in. I'd imagine myself above a tight ass, wearing my new sneakers, the feel of hot sex surrounding my cock and the pressure on my toes as they crunched the rubber soles into the mattress. Then I'd toss my load into the sneaker I'd stuffed my cock down, blasting streams of cum deep inside. The next morning, I'd wear those sneakers to work, hotter than blazes thinking about the secret treasure the left one contained from the night before. That would be exciting enough for me to take the uninitiated partner and balance things out later that night. But I still hadn't found a man who lusted after sneaker sex.

If only shoe outlets were cruise joints! The staff at the local Foot Depot started calling me "Sneaker Man." As soon as I'd walk in, they'd be showing off the new lines. As the count of sneakers in my closet soared past 600 pair, I redesigned a storage room to hold them all! The only thing I needed to get a hard on would be walking in and taking a few deep breaths, then I'd prop my feet up so I could look at and feel the rubber treads while I soloed. All the while, I kept looking for more ways to find men that felt like I did. Rock videos, track and field events, magazine advertisements, sports posters, I tossed over them all. By now, I'd all but given up on the bars.

It was technology that finally gave me the answer...the first day I logged onto the Internet. Once I got the double slash dot com thing worked out, I started running searches for shoe companies and sneaker manufacturers. There are a lot of them...plenty of hot sneaker pictures to download and print out, but no models. Of course there was the one thing I'm now sure everyone uses the Internet for: cruising! I jumped right to search mode and into the UseNet Newsgroups, where I started under the simple string of "Sneakers." Sit back and wait, about a dozen popped up, a lot of the web sites I've already browsed, lots of sportswear entries. From the look of it, it was all G-Rated and nothing sexual. I decided, rather than chew against my online time, I'd capture this info and read through it later. I knocked the sneakers I'd piled on top of the printer to the floor and ran off a hard copy.

I was rolling my cock back and forth across the wavy treads of an old wrestling sneaker when my eyes just about bugged out. The first entry on the list I'd just printed was a header for "Charlie's Sneaker Pages". Even though I'd signed off less than a couple hours ago, I had to get back online right away! My hands were shaking so bad that my point'n clicking kept missing the icons and I had to settle myself down. When I finally quit jittering enough to type, I entered the code and got the happy homepage surprise of my life. A multiple sneaker listing of old advertisements for sneakers through the decades and a list of best and worst. Also, a list of other potential resources, including an alt.clothing.sneakers discussion group...wow! I pulled my clicker right to that one and felt a squeeze of pre-cum when I saw the following message board from guys looking for "Sneaker Sex". I clicked it right away, and was soon hooked up to exactly what I was always looking for.

There, in glorious color, was a sneaker contact board and addresses for men into sneakers. There weren't that many, but it was still more than I'd ever seen. Pictures, too...some just stolen off the manufacturers' boards but also shots that other men had posted from movies and TV shows or advertisements for other products, and of the men themselves, standing in leather jackets and high tops, or nothing more than sneakers and a smile, and best yet, a man with rubber shorts and a pair of canvas low cuts. My cock went right to full attention. He was on the boards and his return address was there, so I typed him a brief message.

Whispering a prayer, I sent it on its way.

The next morning just about broke my brain. There was no "new mail" message for me before I left for work, so I went to my office and spent the entire day fidgeting, wondering if I'd be hearing back from my mystery man. I rubbed the heels of my sneakers together so I could feel the heat in my heels and listen to the friction squeak between a pair of hot, white rubber soles. I raced home, nervous as a college pledge. This time, the "new mail" light WAS on, and I zipped straight into my mail box. Not only was there a name and number in the message, but two hot file pictures from this man, dressed in full body rubber and wearing red runners. His cock was hanging out from the pants in one shot, the other was his ass in tight rubber shorts, shirtless back and beautiful multicolored sneakers, all racing away from the camera. That was the deal for me, I would've fucked him right there if I could've jerked him through the screen and into my workroom.

Judging from the misspellings in his return message, he was as hyped up as I was. I typed in a response and sent it off, the next morning there was one from him. We kept this up for a few weeks, telling each other how we'd jerk ourselves off with and into our sneaker collections. He had only forty pair so far, but claimed that he'd toss his load into each sneaker at least three times before allowing himself another pair. We exchanged fantasies for a few more months until he told me that business would be bringing him near my city, if he rented a car, could he spend a weekend with me?

His phone number and name were included in the last message. We set the date that night, and I started crossing off the days on my calendar.

The evening the doorbell rang, I was ready. He arrived in a loose fitting jogging suit, which I immediately ordered him to take off. "Turn around," I demanded, "I want a better look." He begins to present himself, dressed pretty much as his picture on the board suggested. Rubber shorts, rubber t-shirt, wool socks and a smart pair of black vinyl sneakers with dark rubber side lining. "Get the shorts off and follow me."

Bad Sneakers

I lead him back to my study where I had a wooden chair waiting for him, along with several pieces of clothesline. I push his shoulders into the back support and pull his hands around behind, tying them together with the first piece of clothesline. Pulling his legs along the sides of the seat, I tied his ankles in place to the chair's back legs, lifting the thick black rubber treads of his sneakers in full view. It also forces him forward, moving his cock and balls into a spot where they become easier to get at!

Once I had him in place and ready, I choose my weapons, a pair of dark blue sneakers with white sidelining, the edges well worn from both wear and play. I pulled up my office chair and sat across from him, putting just a drop of lube on my finger. I teased the tip of his juicy cock, smearing the precious dollop around the cock head and along the slit, slicking it up for his coming footwork. Rolling my chair a couple of feet away, I propped my sneakers up on the seat of his chair and rested the treads of my sneakers against his ready for action cock.

The heels of my sneakers pressed against his balls and I sandwich the inside arches in a herringbone hole on opposite sides of his cock. Then I began to rock, with his cock trapped between the gummy sides of my sneakered feet. I haven't put any lube on the shaft yet, so all he gets to feel is pulling and pushing. This is no stroke for him, just me tugging, trapped as he is by my bondage and feet. I can tell how surprised he is, I know he was expecting to get jerked off into a sneaker, the way we described our solo sessions to each other over the net. When he told me that he always wanted to be restrained when someone else gave him sneaker sex, I doubt that this was anything near what he had envisioned.

He loves it. He groans and struggles against his ropes, trying to make his captured cock slide around between my sneakered feet. "No dice, man. You stay in my chair, I move at my pace. This is just the beginning." I pressed the treads of my sneakers into his balls and arch my toes back, giving that cock a real hard stretch before letting go. Scooping a crepe soled CVO from my collection; I jam it over his erect cock and observe how it stands away from his hips, like a size nine shoe condom.

Moving behind him, I start rocking myself while staring at the treads of his athletic shoes and the white clothesline holding them in place. By looking down his chest, I can see the top of his sneaker covered cock, bobbing as he tries to keep contact against the wells of his sneaker. His heavy breathing and happy moans are making me burn as well!

I get my cock above his bound wrists and between the slats of the chair back, rubbing against his skin. Physical contact gets both of us more excited, his breathing keeps speeding up as he humps away at the sneaker covering his cock. I decide that I want his sperm shooting between my feet, so I back away from where I've been heating myself up. But first, I want to go to the kitchen for a beer.

When I come back, he's hornier than ever, helpless to get that final tumbler loose in his balls. He wants to toss his load so bad that he's growling between his moans, a sound so wild that even I have to stop and listen while I watch his frenzied thrusts. I sit across from him again and stare him down as he glares at me, almost daring me to get him off. Yet I'm the one who put him in this position!

That's enough for me. I crack my beer and take a few swallows, then lift the sneaker from his reddening cock. "You want to toss your load off?"

"Oh yeah, coach. Give it to me, man."

Calling me coach! That wasn't in his fantasy e-mails! I'm going to save that one for the next encounter, that's for sure. For now, though, I take a handful of Crisco and smear it between and around the rubber in the arches of my sneakers while he watches. "You ready to hump my sneaks?" His eyes are glazing as he watches me greasing up the slit between my feet. He knows what's coming and he's ready to beg. His ass and balls push their way up as far as the edge of the chair and his restraints will allow.

Bad Sneakers

A couple more swigs of my beer and I'm ready to watch him work for it. I lean back and prop my feet back on the chair in the position we started out in, his cock between my sneakers, sandwiching him in the greasy hole between my feet. He absolutely howls with excitement. I pick up the sneaker I'd stuffed on his cock earlier and ram it over mine, his pre-cum slicked up the base where his struggles spread his juices inside. I'm ready to rock his socks off, and turn mine out, too.

Gentle at first, evenly rolling his cock up and down against my sneakers while humping my own sneaker insulated cock, I listen to his grunts and groans. Every so often, I paused and took another swallow from my beer as I listened to his wordless pleas to cum, his body jerking and twisting at the greasy space surrounding his cock. I continue pumping away till I decide enough is enough. He's been wanting to cum for a while now, but I've gotten so damn fired up that I wanna blow my own load!

I pull my sneakers away from his cock ("Coaaaaaaach!") and slather another blob of Crisco in the rubbered center spaces, and while I'm at it, a quick palmful on my own cock before we bring this monster to a spitting close. I ram my cock deep into the greasy insole of my solo sneaker, then jam the heel balls of my sneakered feet into his human balls, crushing his cock inside the hot spot between the footwear. That's when I really let him have it...I begin pumping my feet like I'm on a bicycle, left then right. It's like playing piano pedals and it gets my man screaming in sneaker ecstasy.

"Oh yeah, coach, play ball on me! Get my cum on that hot sneaker, get me all over that rubber sole! Do it to me Coach, do it to me! Yaagghhh..."

That does it! I'm pumping away like an Olympic cyclist at the same time I'm humping at the sneaker between my legs, and I can see him blasting away, his cum spraying away on the canvas vamps of my sneakered feet. Inside my single sneaker, my enclosed cock starts pounding and pulsing, tossing shot after shot of my own hot semen against the insole! I'm jamming both my feet into his balls as I arch back and let my balls explode, giving me my own ecstatic release.

It takes a while for both of us to return to Earth, and when we do, he gives me a broad smile. His hair is in a sweaty tangle on his head and his face is dripping wet. And all he can ask is "Coach, can we please replay that last one again sometime?"

My smile flashes back at him as I reply "I've got over 1,000 pair of sneakers in the house. We've got plenty of games to play."

THE FOREST RANGER AND
THE EARTH DADDY

When you're sent up into these mountains for eight months at a time, you think at the beginning that it is going to be paradise. Just you, nature, a microwave dish to keep contact with civilization and all the time in the world. You're going to get back in touch with nature and write the next great American novel. The next Henry David Fucking Thoreau.

Yeah, right.

You do get in touch with nature. Or more like nature gets in touch with you. Paradise fantasies never include insects. Whatever bears are in your dreams aren't the ones that trash your garbage bins and shred your sleeping bag looking for cookie crumbs. Let's face it... this little outpost in the middle of the Rockies is outright lonely. The lonely handful of hikers that stop and chat are welcome, and I'm almost always horny from lack of company. When that sun goes low enough for me to make one last sweep of the horizon and the temperature cools down a bit, it doesn't take long for me to pull on some rubber gear and relax. Even before I left Texas for this job, I knew there were some things I couldn't live without.

Among the usual necessary clothing and amusements, I packed one dry suit, one set of tight exercise pants and shirt, and because I knew I'd need them for more practical purposes, boots galore. The National Park Service is pretty generous although basic. You get rain gear, more boots (!), five uniforms and accouterments (two sets of handcuffs and a pistol/rifle/ammo, badge, etc.), a place to live, food delivered, a two way radio and - welcome to the modern world - a cellular phone with fax attachments.

I have a very nominal set of directives. First, take care of the park area! So I look out for fires, watch the weather monitors, keep my eyes out for trouble and maintain the trail-grounds. The other is to take care of the people that might pass through on this path, and since my turf was pretty remote… I chose it for that reason... they are the few and the dedicated. What I didn't think about was that eight months in the Rockies was asking to take a vow of celibacy. But that makes the part about taking care of the hikers take on a whole new fantastic dimension sometimes.

Once, about two months into my tour of duty, my storm tracker picked up on a heavy duty thunder basher coming into my zone. Just my luck, a solo hiker makes it to my cabin during the same afternoon. One hundred twenty days of nothing but my imagination and gear for company, and a scruffy trail buff comes by. I was in my cabin fetching out some boots and rain gear, and I warn him of the impending storm. I am more than glad for the company, because even though I have a radio (skipped the TV...given the chance, wouldn't you take a summer without sitcoms?), keeping up with news and world events is a dodgy proposition. So I put on my boots, started up the coffee kettle and invited him to wait out the coming rains.

I didn't miss the way his eyes stayed for a more than necessary glance on my knee-highs, either.

When the thunderheads did break, it was a dandy. One of those bright lightning flash/ crash of immediate thunder type storms that can make you very appreciative of Nature's force and what an all-powerful bitch she can be when the conditions are right. While Terry (I had since learned his name) and I chatted over coffee, the storm water slammed the walls outside my small government issued cabin. And like most storms of this intensity, after passing through this part of the mountains, it hurried off to its next destination, leaving well filled washes and a steady drizzle behind.

"This is the period I like the best," Terry told me, "because the Earth really opens up for you."

"In what way," I responded.

The Forest Ranger And The Earth Daddy

"The smells and textures," my hiking friend replied. "Clean rain water lets you explore the ground, to inhale our planet's soulful ness, to actually rub yourself against it. If you really have your feelings in tune on a day like this one, you can almost feel yourself taking roots in the ground itself. After all, that's why you came here, isn't it?"

I had to admit, he had me pegged. More than that, he had my attention. Like most hard core hiking enthusiasts, Terry's body was solid, but not meaty. He had black curly hair and a thick, wild moustache, accented by several days of unshaved beard, offset by the calmest, most tranquil brown eyes I think I'd ever seen. He was also very hairy, gritty arm and chest hair plainly visible against his t-shirt, which clung to his chest, muscled enough to testify to his strength and still managing to show the bones below. I didn't ask his age, but I would've guessed early forties to my mid-thirties. There was also the way he kept lingering those eyes on my ranger boots. I had to be careful with my undercurrent of desire...I kept thinking of that moustache pressing down hard against them. Or better yet, his accepting them from me and putting them on himself.

Which is exactly what he asked about next!

"I saw the row of boots against the wall there," he asked, "and I've always enjoyed hiking in a good pair of sturdy rubbers. Do you mind if I look them over?" Oh, shit, I thought...did he just say what I thought I heard? Or was my over stimulated imagination filling in too many blanks? I told Terry to go ahead and look, I had to go out quickly and make some observations for wildfires and any storm damage before phoning in an evening report. I sucked in my breath and all but jumped out the door into the remains of the drizzle.

A hasty scan of my weather monitors showed that the storm was clearly heading down the valley, and a sweep of the mountains indicated no fires, so all was well. With the exception of the hormonal storm that was now reaching full niner in my system. I wanted to pull my uniform off, throw it outside to the mud and leaves and find this man in my cabin waiting for me "with nothing more than a pair of my boots on! The initial impulse was resisted, even if my cock was telegraphing my instincts.

I went back to hook up my phone and let my control post know that my sector was undamaged, to find Terry fondling a shin high pull-up boot. "I love this one," he said with a gleam in his eye. "Perfect for kicking up some mulch, don't you think?" If I had any questions left, they were gone then and there. "Put them on if they fit; they're a size 10. I've got to make a call." I was in my office like a flash, phoned in the most comprehensive under ten minute report known to the Park Service and out in time to see Terry, standing there in full splendor with no more than my green and yellow thick rubber waders. His body was fully proportional to his height, strong but not exaggerated.

"Well, my young ranger friend, would you like to go outside and experience what nature has gifted us with today?"

There was nothing more that I wanted to try. My uniform was gone, replaced by my rubber athletic pants. My smooth, semi-naked body was outside behind his as twilight began to settle in under the receding storm clouds. Terry was already splashing water from a two inch deep puddle area not far from my cabin. Leaves and drainage were flying playfully as he aimed a splash at me. "Come here, barefoot boy," he motioned. I didn't need to be told twice.

He pressed his chest against my back, his moustache tickling my neck as his tongue slid along my shoulder. He held me as we gently went to our knees, he in boots, me in rubber shorts, his hands and arms pressing me down towards the pool of rainwater and earth beneath us.

"I want you to lie in it," he said. "Press yourself into it, let it take you in. Feel my weight on yours, sense the Earth beneath you." I followed his instructions, all the while completely aware of his wet body entwined with mine, the mud against my chest, the rubber against my groin, the boots weaving around my legs. Terry continued in the same low, commanding voice, "As I hold you, young man, and you feel my sex pressing against and into you, feel your own spirit and sex taking root in the core of the Earth's being."

He reached into the mud on either side of us and smeared thick handfuls across the hairy mass of his chest. "The Earth is a god with gifts to offer us, foremost of which is pleasure." He pressed himself back against me, using his full weight now. I could feel his rock hard cock aligning to the ass-groove of my rubber shorts, as my chest sank deeper into the mud and natural compost directly below me.

With each motion of his chest and torso, I could feel the leafy paste soaking into my back from off the front of his body. The mud and sticks were scratching at my shoulders. My own nipples turning solid in the supple clay I was shifting in, a little deeper with each of his strokes. As gritty as I thought the mud should have been, it actually felt lubricating. Terry continued with his sensual stroking, the heat between us building. He paused again, to gather more of the earthy mix of mountain and rain, and pile it onto my back. "It feels better than you thought it would, doesn't it?" he whispered.

Another handful went onto his head, covering his facial hair and pulling at the curls of hair along his forehead. It was almost as if he was putting on a mask, it transformed him so much. Terry covered from his hairline to his waist in the dark ground of my mountain outpost, rainwater and sweat dripping from his muscles and body fur, his face almost a tribal shield of mud and leaves. "I search for kindred spirits every time I hike these trails, but I usually have to seek the most remote locations," he told me. "Your willingness to come outside and play speaks to the little boy I can see inside of you." Terry gathered up another scoop of mud and held it over me. "Here. Get this inside those rubber pants and against your body."

He moved away from me so I could rise from the pool we had been rolling in. I got to my knees, and he put his fist down the back of my shorts. His fingers uncurled and the gooey debris seeped against the skin tight recesses available between my rubber and skin. I groaned with pleasure. Terry's hand smoothed the mulch along my ass, taking the time to work some into the space between my cheeks, even letting some touch against my asshole.

I was no longer capable of speaking back at this man, who was catching my imagination as a shaman with each word and gesture. That sensation of mud against my hole... there was nothing at all to compare it to. As Terry continued to move his hand inside my rubber shorts, his free hand went for another handful of Rocky Mountain silt to press against my chest.

My own identity was moving away from me. I was no longer a fair skinned, horny uniformed Park Ranger employed by the government. Terry was transforming me into a randy wood-sprite, a sexually playful imp rolling in the clay of my mountainside. He had become a mud covered spiritual mentor, an Earth Daddy guiding me in rubber boots through my first true communication with the sensuality of the forest. Both of his hands were now in use, both at my chest, keeping the elements alive on my body and my nipples keenly aware of his presence.

The silt he had covered my ass with had worked its way to the front of my rubber shorts, where I could feel my cock and balls reacting accordingly. The sounds I uttered were no longer human. They came from a space deep within, as Terry's mud covered moustache and tongue once again sought the pit of my neck, and the boots rode against my legs.

"Go down, my young friend. Place your spirit into the hands of Nature." I laid myself back into the molding, liberating fit of the Earth and let it surround my body once more.

The sun had fallen below the horizon and the clouds had dissipated, leaving the sky clear for the moon and first light of stars. Terry's voice took on a rawer tone as his breathing rate increased. The mud he had slathered across his body was caking onto mine and I could feel his solid dick pressing into the crack of my ass. Water and mud were rippling and splattering into my face and hair in a pattern that only nature could contrive, and I realized that Terry was right. Pinned between the soft, fertile ground and his firm muscular body, I was divining a muddy link with Earth and man sex.

It was obvious that my energy was funneling into Terry, because just as I felt those first muddy crashing waves of orgasm shooting through me, he ground his balls into the small of my back, and pinning my arms to my sides, shot his hot seed across the cool, earthy mulch that his desires had coated me with.

He rolled off of me panting as I turned on my side to face him, my rubber shorts full of my own seed. I took that sweaty mustached face, enhanced by the remains of the storm's debris, and drove my tongue deep into Terry's mouth.

With both of us still feeling the comforting cradle of mud beneath us, he returned the gesture, two as one for Earth below.

BRUSHFIRE

Every time there is a storm in the mountains, I have to run to my observation points. Although it doesn't happen very often, a lightning bolt can quickly touch off a wildfire. It's my job to spot these thin plumes of smoke before they get to anything more than a couple of burning dead trees. Most times, a storm passes through without incident, and I can put on some rubber pants and roll around in the mud, reminding myself of Terry, the hiker who visited in the rain here in the deep woods of my station. It's always a good way to release some tension.

Then there was the one episode that every Ranger dreads....

In the six month of my tour of duty, in what was proving to be a long hot summer, my storm tracker picked up a new set of thunderheads moving in my direction. This wasn't going to be just a passing storm, but one that would roll directly over my private mountain, snapping licks directly at my cabin. Not that I'm the Cowardly Lion, but crashes of thunder that don't separate from their parenting bolt stir up old childhood fears. Almost like the skin crawling sensation from a B-grade sci-fi episode. I could see from my screen that this storm was going to be one of those.

Nature did not disappoint me. There was thirty minutes of brutal rain, accompanied by the most viscous, violent lightning that the trees could draw. I was worried from the moment the storm started, because this lightning was going from air to ground, not from cloud to cloud, and as dry as the mountain had been, it was a recipe for disaster. As soon as things settled even slightly, I was at my observation post scouting for strikes. There were two. One was on the other side of the valley, contained in a small alcove along the river, it would be easy enough to put out with an aerial drop. The second however was directly down the trail, maybe five miles tops...from me. My radio was still crackling with residual static when I squeezed my mike switch and said with my knuckles turning white, "I have an impending situation here..."

We're trained not to panic. We're drilled to remain calm. But when you see a wisp of smoke down wind from where you live, even the Terminator would get a case of nerves. Base gave me the standard set of instructions, and I began carrying them out... turn on my tracking beacon for the chopper to find, put on my protective gear and wait for support.

I pulled from my rack a specially treated pair of proximity pants, boots, jacket and hood. Although I knew that it would be a few minutes before a 'copter could get over the rise and a man could get to me, every second seemed essential. I checked my tube tank for oxygen, even though I had given it my regular inspection glance that morning. I fastened the hose to the respirator of my D.S.Parks regulation Breather Mask. As I slid the mask over my neck and snapped the shiny hood in place over my head, I glanced out for the helicopter and listened for its arrival. With only a few minutes passing since I had made the initial distress call, I could already see the flecks of orange lapping flames at the base of the valley below.

Then I heard a noise that couldn't have sounded sweeter. The chunka-chunk of rotor blades approached as three helicopters moved along the edge of the valley. While I watched and listened to my radio, I witnessed the first attempt at retarding the spread of the brushfire. A curtain of water cascaded from air to surface while I listened for the radio's response that the flames had been extinguished on the first pass.

I was not in luck.

It was easy to see that the bone dry forest bed was ready fodder for a wildfire; lines of orange popped out almost immediately and began creeping up the mountain in my direction. "Prepare to take emergency cover," my radio snapped. "Second-man coming in now."

Brushfire

Two of the three helicopters reversed course and headed back for more water, while the third moved in towards my station. There was no way they could lift me out, but they could drop another person in. If the ladder could get within ten or twenty feet of the ground, an emergency man could leap down and we'd make a run for it based on what he saw from overhead.

The man who fell to earth took the drop with skill, rolling with his landing like a gymnast. He sprang up from his tumble, racing like a bull towards my cabin. Even with his gear, I could tell this was a man with a solid body. I threw open the door, and before he was even inside, I could hear him yelling.

"My name is Chris. The fire is too close to secure your cabin, we've got to take cover now!"

Smoke was rolling thick through the trees as Chris grabbed my jacket. "Is there a drainage stream or culvert nearby" he shouted. I indicated that there was one a few hundred yards away, a cement double pipe that a small stream flowed under the trail. "There's not much time!" He pulled me by my collar out the door, oxygen masks askew on our faces. I know as well as any emergency worker that you can't outrun a wildfire, the best you can do is take shelter. I led Chris down the hill, even as the flames raced towards us, to where a twin sized drainpipe let a small mountain stream gurgle under the footpath. The fires were just yards away from us now, we could feel the heat blowing towards us as we pushed into the four by eight space and hoped for the best.

The stream was running a bit faster than usual, thanks to the storm's runoff, fortunately for us. But weeks of dry weather, hot winds and no precipitation had done its work. The forest floor was a carpet of dry tinder and even though dampened by the thunderstorm, the fire chewed right through it without hesitation. The flames sucked air into its vortex so fast that the drainpipe sounded like a wind tunnel. Chris and I huddled together, hoping the concrete and stream water would protect us as the literal snapping roar of fire began its pass over us. We clung to each other for what seemed like forever, but in the case of any wildfire, was just a matter of a few minutes. I knew that my cabin was built to resist burning, but the train like howl above us kept me mindful of nature's wrath. With Chris's strong arms around me, I could feel both our hearts racing. It wasn't until the sounds of danger had passed that I realized he hadn't loosened his grip.

There was no more roar, none of the intensity of nearby heat. Yet neither of us had budged. There was a different kind of heat now.

Chris moved his hand wordlessly beneath my protective jacket, his palm against the skin of my chest. When had he taken his gloves off, I wondered. His fingers flicked between the jacket's cloth like lining and my hardening nipples. Too soon for me, I was concerned for my cabin. But I still didn't move. The breathing under my oxygen mask quickened, and his hands had discovered what I always knew...my tits were hot wired to my crotch. A low moan escaped the space behind my mask, his fingers intensified their exploration of my body. The air smelled of charred wood and steam, and in the tight zone of safety Chris and I had sought, the scent of sexual musk was starting to manifest itself.

His hand moved down my waist, slipping below my beltline. I arched from his first touch of my pubic hairs, the tingle of lust was breaking down my concern for my cabin. Chris's hands were cold from the runoff water we were sheltered in, and a small moan again passed through my lips. I heard him chuckle as his muscles tightened their grip around my chest. Even with our bodies bent almost double, he was strong enough to maneuver me underneath him, straightening us out until he had his bulk on top of me, turning my body into a barricade against the water trying to stream through the tunnel we, such a short time ago, were huddling in. The heavy breathing behind his face mask was coming out jagged and rough, and suddenly I felt his hand pulling my pants away from my ass. I shouted... but not in horror. Chris must not have realized it, but the run-off was up to my shoulders, and when it got a chance to pour around my exposed dick, it was ice cold! That was enough to turn my heat off and get out towards the pipe's opening.

"I'm sorry," he grunted.

To his obvious surprised delight, I answered that it was okay, it was just that the water down my crotch had pulled me back to ground zero. Chris arched an eyebrow.

"Well then," he said, "let's check for damages and continue from there!" He took his helmet and mask away and for the first time, I got a good look at my rescuer's face. His hair was cut tight and close and his eyes flashed eagerness. I knew there would be no turning this man down. He was one who was used to getting his way. After we made sure there were no lingering damages then raking over any lingering hot spots, I radioed my assessment of the situation then turned in my seat to see Chris, who had stripped down to what was definitely not regulation wear. Standing before me with nothing more than his reflective jacket was a gym-bull of a man, his deep eyes burning and a dick ready to start a few fires of its own. "You look good in silver. Show me what you look like without it."

Once I was naked, he took his hand and gave his bull balls an assertive pull. "I just saved your ass, boy. Get over here and show me some appreciation."

Chris had the muscles of a competition bodybuilder. As he spread the flaps of his jacket open, the slightest smile played across his stern face. Radio messages from the chopper teams filled in the background as they dropped their second and third loads on the blaze that was now miles up the mountain.

I put my hands against Chris's solid steel thighs. My rescuer had some flames of his own that needed to be extinguished, and I was prepared to give him the hero's welcome of a lifetime. He wrapped his heavy, reflective slicker around my head, forcing both the smells of his own musk and smoky rubber into my nostrils as my tongue took its first taste of that sexy tool. If the copters had to make that many passes to put out a brushfire, I knew I had plenty of time to thank this particular fire fighter.

BLAINE

"Why is my eagerness to serve him something he thought less important than submission in total?"

"Why all this constant grousing about being a man?" Blaine asked me. "Even a gay man has it better than most of the population in this country. For Christ's sake, you're all but born with a silver spoon between your legs and you're whining that no-one will let you be who you want to be!"

The conversation had spun out of control quite a ways back, as they always seemed to when Blaine and I spoke. I had my own set of clichés that I despised, he had his. Yet he was the closest friend I had who could or wanted to follow my track when discussing more than sports and weather, or who's body was hotter in what movie in a given genre and year, or why Aero Smith was a better 70's dance band than The Commodores. Blaine was one of but a few voices in an ocean of conformity, and one of the few friends I could depend upon to not spend countless wasted words on gay speak.

He'd even relayed it to me one morning after a rubber session when I finally asked him "What is it you see in me?"

Blaine had to stop for a second. His key ceased jiggling in the padlock for a moment, his eyes moved away from the bedpost and to my still hooded face. His big brown eyes narrowed to a squint as he pondered the question. I was sure he knew his answer as soon as I asked, but he would never allow himself the appearance of being able to spike me with too ready a reply. His answer started out slow, then picked up momentum when he was certain of his words. "In the morning after we wake up from a night of hard, satisfying rubber-sex," he began, "I never have to be afraid of you not having something to say. I know that the first thing out of your mouth won't be some idiotic blather...or worse yet, that you won't have anything at all to say. Sometimes I may accuse you of thinking too much, but I'll never accuse you of insufficient thinking. There have been many desperate evenings when I've woke up to a morning's worth of self questioning about how this... thing…got into my bed. Jim, I've gone to bed with more than my share of stupid men. But not you, you, well are never stupid."

Of course I love him, and have for the past seventeen years. The ties between Blaine and I are more spiritual than anything else, our mutually conflicting schedules prevent our paths from crossing in any more than a few months each year.

Here I am then, again given the chance to stare into the most sexual eyes I've ever known and give in to the most thoroughly in control man I've ever met. In the life that I have lived so far, I tally Blaine on the small finger count of friends that truly matter, a man who is as much kinsman as Master. Yet even now we were engaged in the kind of argumentative exercise that he loves drawing me into. I've often felt that this was just as much a testing of my limits as anything he ever tried in a scene.

"Fuck being 'servile'!" Blaine was roaring away at me over some off the cuff comment I'd made about slaving. "That's just pretending! Deep down inside you want to be a Man with another Man. If someone isn't letting you be what you really want to be or what you really are, get the hell away from him, because he's just slumming for a blowjob. Only if your balls are in danger of exploding unless you con a trick into a night of horny sex, don't pretend for anybody!" He placed his head in his hands for a moment to catch his breath and gather his thoughts. Then he looked up from his seat at me. "Jim, today we will take a special journey together. I know we've gone off on some ingenious pathways before, but this time we'll make some stops along the route. I think there are some things we should try to explain to each other."

I have to admit, what Blaine was trying to say at first eluded me. There had never been a session with him, from our initial meeting when he handcuffed me to a bed with a rubber sheet stretched out tight beneath me, to the last time we saw each other in a New York City hotel during a mutual cross while traveling, that hadn't been anything less than a dual epiphany. "I'm ready, Sir."

"Then strip."

These are the words that mark the beginning, the transition. Blaine gives me that simple two word command and our bond shifts from an equidistant orbit given of friendship to the teetering balance of an erotic fulcrum, a delicately shared geometric formula based on elaborate sexual equations. I shed my clothes directly and await my next order, already feeling those inner doors emerging from behind their barricades.

"The same rules as always, Jim, with one new directive. Answer all questions fully and without hesitation. Follow commands as you always have, with your usual obedience." Blaine removed his shirt and wrapped his arms around me, compressing me in his grip.

"Get on your knees and hold me," Blaine ordered. I did so without question. "Now tell me. Isn't this comfortable? Don't you feel like you belong here?"

"Yes Sir," I replied, my arms around his calves. "It feels like the only place I should be."

His hand stroked through my hair. "Do you feel like any less of a man because you're on your knees?"

"No Sir, not with you."

My head jerked back as Blaine pulled my hair down, forcing my face to stare up at his. "That's the whole point. Anytime you submit without surrender, you can't be a whole man, you're only playing a role. Stop trying to be Mister Best Boy and learn that for every time you give into a strong Master, the two of you are Men in Love for the duration of your scene because of the levels of your interactions. This is adult sexual contact. It is about spirit, not fakery, it is about who we are, not a costume or a 'play character.' It's about my desire to let you just fucking uncork and submit,

damn you. I don't want you on your knees with an 'A+ slave' attitude, I want you on your knees because you know you belong
there and want to be there."

He backed away from me and I went into proper stance,
eyes down, hands behind. Blaine returned with a rubber collar and
two wrist restraints, fastening it into place. "Stand."

With a fair amount of difficulty, I pulled myself to my knees,
then balanced myself until I stood, legs splayed, before him. I
heard the cold click of chain links when a support chain was
attached from the ceiling to my collar. As the "hiss" of air squeezed
from a pair of snakebite cups pressed against my nipples, he star-
tled me by asking "Why would you direct so much attention and
affection to a man that for but two or three times a year, you don't
even see?"

Through the first tantalizing wet tingles of suction, I replied,
"Sir, if you wonder why this boy waxes enthusiasm in your direction, it's because he believes in the concept of extended families.
It isn't the proximity of the man but his qualities. So even if we may
be on the opposite sides of the continent, my fondness for you
need not be constrained by my ability to see or be touched. My
greatest fear in life is to actually end a relationship as close as I
feel for you in the manner where the final line, 'He thinks of me as
him,' is the epitaph of what you remember."

My nipples distended into their rubber confines as I continued. "There are too many exceptional people, of which YOU are
one, who contribute to my life in such strongly positive ways that I
work hard to not let that happen. Again, I think of you often and in
warm manners. What ever links of spirituality my body challenges
me with, you are a link to my family here on Earth and as such,
one of the people I consider as a close kin, a brother, a Mentor
and friend."

Through the duration of my answer, Blaine was sliding a
rubber ring over my cock and balls with a fireman's boot set at the
end of a short tether. When he was finished, he gave it a bat and
left the boot swaying between my legs. "You'll always have that,

Jim," he answered. "Even if I care enough about you to want to see you getting more. Each of us needs to find kindred spirits in this world that we have 'dealt with' ironically... Honesty is the rush. My friendships and contacts in these areas are limited deliberately so I can invest an appropriate amount of time in the 'right' friends. I manage to do well by those I care for. I want you to know clearly that for me, 'dominant' is a very rich facet of who I am. It is complete and very deeply part of me. I don't 'play games'. I just am what I am. That's what makes the sex good and powerful."

"Most Tops don't know how to do what I am talking about. It takes a lot of experience and heart to learn, and honesty. But I find that few men are spiritually ready for the level of intensity and eroticism that I want and expect. This is the reason both why my stable is so small, less than you can count on one hand, and why you have been admitted. I knew early on, in my gut, seventeen years ago, you were ready for this and could understand it. It's why I reject cruelty and the vicious abuse that some 'Tops' dish out. I'll admit, I can be sadistic, but it takes a hell of a bottom with a powerful spirit to bring it out in me. When it happens, the sadism always reconciles in a flood of emotion and protectiveness."

That was not a declaration I ever expected to hear anyone, including Blaine, convey during the course of a session. Even one as odd as this. "Protectiveness, Sir?"

"Jim, it's not about 'Top' and 'bottom' but shared power of soul in a very elegant and erotic exchange. A minute of sorts. The power of both must be present or it doesn't work. Period."

"The music or the dance, Sir?"

"Probably both, Jim. I would more simply say that the whole encounter is a ritual in nature, and the act of ritual is for both parties to 'cross over' into a sacred space where deeper elements of life may be expressed. A ritual by definition has an end, and the point is for you to realize inner levels of strength. I ask you...what is your definition of humiliation?"

A blindfold covered my eyes, taking away my visual connection to the scene, increasing my reliance in Blaine. Wherever he was leading me, I was now dependent on his descriptions of the immediate world to retain an understanding of its form. As meager a departure as it may seem, it forced me to pay stricter attention to the tonic of his voice as he continued to describe his thoughts. I drew a deep breath and answered "To go through the motions when deeper feelings are present and could be touched and engaged?"

A slow caress of Blaine's fingers along my ribs raised gooseflesh and indicated that my answer pleased him. "Why do I often wear boots in a scene?" Blaine slapped the fireman's boot dangling between my legs and I groaned, for him. Continuing as the boot swung back and forth off my balls, "It symbolizes the Master, grounded by gravity, must remain in the real world of safe sex and protection and care for his charge." I could hear the rattle of a metal stand being wheeled next to me, then recognizing it as the holder of Blaine's suspended bright red water bladder. Its narrow hose was slipped into the boot off my crotch and I listened while Blaine clicked open the valve at the underside of the sack. A gradual trickling of fluid began to fill the boot, a slowly timed weight dragging my ball sack towards the floor.

"You are correct in that what I speak of takes time, but the time is worth it. The fundamental issue is that I won't accept role playing because I am too experienced and too old for it. I want a man to be ready to submit, to be at my feet and be IN that state. I want him to feel owned, possessed, and ultimately free of ego/personality. I can GIVE you that, Jim. Why should I...or you...accept less?"

Grunting through this new pulling at my groin, I gasped "I know why I accept 'less' on many occasions. It's called loneliness. I've tried a couple of times to break off relationships when they feel 'forced.' Yet there's a very basic part of my psyche that pushes everything out of the way at times. That's why, when a Master calls, my submissiveness overwhelms my rationale and I go. The part of me that desires and needs the bondage and S/M just can't be denied. Surrendering to you, Sir, is always easy enough, because I already have great respect for your ideas and for you as an intellect."

The time and gravity comments were not lost. Blaine's simple slow torture mechanism of the boot and water made me aware that if I allowed myself to give up concentrating on how it was happening as opposed to understanding how it worked, then one more fragment of my ego dropped away and his desires moved that much closer to the fore. Yet I still hadn't organized my thoughts enough to comprehend why my eagerness to serve him was something he thought less important than submission in total.

"Getting myself beyond that is the challenge. I'm not sure who faces the greater chore here," I told him. "You by leading me to a point where the ego breaks off or me giving up to where I become unafraid enough to make the leap."

"The 'leap' is a big one, you are correct. But it's the one gift I can give you. An ability to see your deeper primal masculine self, meet him, if you will, without all the fucking background noise. If you go through the motions and do all the 'Sir' and 'Master' stuff superficially, you've gone through something that is as safe as an amusement park ride. I hate to admit it, but I can't empathize easily with loneliness because I've been so often pursued. What I can offer you is true strength, peace and calm, and the ability to learn to trust a Man who both protects and demands of you."

"So in effect, I become a part of you for a period of time in order to do and see different things?"

"Yes, Jim. Control is always aimed at the inner man, to allow him something powerful enough to 'believe in' so he can truly surrender inside himself and transcend the nattering of his ego." He popped the yellow rubber of the snakebite cups from my nipples and I sucked my breath in. The warmth of the blood rushing to my chest gave those first deep feelings of pleasure/pain mixture.

"That's hard for me, Sir, because I am one of those men who wants to be the best boy possible."

Blaine had picked up a crop and was flicking it across my swollen nipples. "As long as you are in that headset, though, you are not in submission. You're in aggression. As a result, you can't feel the inner depths of your own strength. You get distracted by 'trying.' I don't want you to 'act' submissive. I want you to know that you can submit to me, progressively, to greater levels of power in yourself." The 'flitflit' of the tip of Blaine's crop took on the mental ticking of a metronome, its time signature attuned from between Master's hand to me, a sightless but sexual journeyman. "Are you strong enough to drop away the shielding and feel the value of being yourself...in my service...without trying to impress me?"

The question was rhetorical, of course. I already knew that Blaine wouldn't be treating me like this if I hadn't impressed him deeply in the first place. Still, the implications of where Blaine was trying to guide me continued eluding me, like an answer written just outside my blindfold. Damn, I needed to reach that point! The pressure of his mental prodding, the gradual increase in physical torments, they kept me struggling toward the endpoint of this particular sensual quest.

With each crack of Blaine's crop, his power over me deepened as my own arousal waxed and waned at his whim. Desires tempted, needed filled, but only as he saw fit to give me. My body trembled with the blows, causing the incremental increasing weight of the filling boot to shift and jostle. Then a realization "You hit my feelings about playing outside of my relationship squarely on the head." I told him. "Despite the degree of 'care taking' being a play slave replenishes, I often feel lousy about myself afterwards and wish for more, even as I treasure the warmth from a strong ass beating. Is it humiliating? Sometimes yes. But when it seems to be the closest thing to an affectionate relationship that I know right then, it becomes...I won't even say difficult...but impossible to ignore."

Almost on cue, Blaine moved form my chest to my ass. He already knows that warm ups are unnecessary in this zone. "I'm not trying to spoil your other contacts! You do and we all do sex sometimes for its own sake. I'm a powerful man," he punctuated the sentence with an uncommonly forceful strike to my backside.

"I've learned from others, earned part of it through experience and also through embarrassing accident. I have my weaknesses and strengths. But others want strength from me and it's erotic to give it."

Pleasing warmth had crept from my buttocks and thighs and into the gray cells of my brain. The power of Blaine's dominance had once again erotically fooled my mind, even though I could already tell that the following morning would bring reds, blacks and blues to my cheeks. I knew that I'd be reminded of his physical touch for the next several days. Mentally, I had the perception that this particular session was already forging a place for the history pages. "Sometimes when I see other men, Sir, the visit is just as much an act as it is an essential need. I always feel the most comfort when I get on my knees for them...yet often I don't 100% mean it. Do you understand what I'm trying to express?"

"I'm trying to tell you that I see you as ready for something more challenging, more erotic. Something that reflects my own deeper sense of why I do this with 'True Men', so hard, by the way, to find. Jim, a True Man knows that giving up and taking in on a spiritual level will always balance, just as soon as you allow it to happen."

"At the same time, Sir, when I tell you what emotional and spiritual levels we sometimes reach, I wonder what and how much I lost or gave up for those moments."

"You alone must do what seems right with each person you include in your sexual life. I'm just telling you who I am and what I know and expect. I use the term 'sacred space' to describe it, simply because it is a place that is accessed by ritual. S/M or BD are highly ritualistic acts, Jim. The contradictions of sex, the 'feeling dirty' leads men to this kind of unwillingness to do it with people who aren't 'THERE' on some serious level."

My blindfold was removed, and Blaine undid the cock ring and boot as well, allowing blood to freely circulate back into my balls and shaft. "What you touch upon in yourself is just, if not even more important, as anything a Master touches in you." His words and my crotch both stabbed like hell. They always did, every time, and from Blaine I lived for it. "Jim, this is what I want you to remember. The people you deal with in the scene are always important." He poured the water from the boot into a near-by basin. When he returned to me, he looked me square in the eye while painfully massaging my nipples. "How many friends have you lost in the past decade?"

"Sir, more than I can count, but everyone one of them still hurts."

"I think that you almost understand what I'm trying to pound into you," he said with an oddly gentle smile. "and I think it's time we moved on." Blaine produced a bag of clothes pins for me to see. "The lesson, Jim, is in letting go. Sometimes we forget that there are still living men standing next to us for every friend we've lost. Don't forget the ones who are gone, but every once in a while, remind yourself to celebrate the living. Remind yourself that there is balance." He lit a pair of candles and set them nearby, then dimmed the electrical lights through the room.

"There are two sides to forever, Jim. The one we exist on now and the one where we discover how far we've moved in time before coming back for the next round."

The first clothespin opened against my already sensitive chest as Blaine gripped the skin with his other hand. "As each pin closes on you, repeat the name of someone you know who has gone."

I felt the tingle as the first pinch came to close. "Wayne, Sir." Second pinch "Ken, Sir." Third "Jan, Sir.". My litany continued on...and on...until a line of clothespins burned clear across my chest, down my midriff and in a circle around my heart. I could no longer control my emotions, each name and clothespin ached so deep that my tears were flowing unceasingly. All I could think of was the ache, the agonizing ache of the losses, and of the respect I had for the man drawing these emotions to skin level.

"All memories of these men are proud ones, Jim. Keep this

next thought in mind; sometimes the longer you let them stay, the more painful their letting go." One by one, starting with the right side of my chest, name-pin after name-pin began coming off as I screamed to the side of forever that Blaine and I represented, tears continuing their free rain. One rubber gloved hand leaving a branded red line up my chest and to my heart, the other gently massaging my cock through the pangs of release, of the letting go. The realization that respect, control and submission remain in the hands of the living, that destiny is still just as much a plan as an accident, that what is power and what is powerful are not always the same. The reminder that the living are meant to be a source of constant celebration even as we mourn our losses.

What ever else Blaine was whispering in my ear at that moment was gone to me, my cries blotting out all other sounds and the flaming ring around my heart branding my nerves straight to the brain, aware now only of the fire in my chest and the slippery, cool hand feverishly stroking my dick. Blaine's hand, in control, guiding me through the tiny point that was/is right now, the pilot of this journey once again taking both of us to a destination only few can understand, accompanied by the explosion from within my balls that shoots across his glove. My sight still blurry as I realize his eyes are also a berth for tears.

My exhausted body fell into his as the warmth of that voice sobbed words of comfort, understanding...and protectiveness. Blaine undid the chain of the collar then released my wrists from the restraints behind my back and led us, spent, to his bed.

If your lawn looks like a brushfire waiting to happen and the yellows of the dandelions out color the blues of your Kentucky...Then you need us! We'll whack your weeds into submission and yank the crabs out from your yard as early as this afternoon. When you need someone hotter than a hose on your driveway, there's no better place to begin than at the

GRASS ROOTS

The ad copy sure read like it was what my yard needed and the accompanying picture was just what my eyes and crotch were looking for. I wondered if all the would-be horticulturists in town looked this amazing! Of course I knew better. If all those ads for "Stud Moving" couldn't possibly be staffed with the husky things in the pictures, neither could the gardening services...or could they? All I knew was I wasn't looking up the phone number for yard care because of blue balls. Too many weeds, not enough time, and my yard was going to Hell. When I had all the time in the world to care for the garden and grass, I had the best yard on the block. Then things started picking up and spare time got diverted into my workday. I could afford the perfect lawn; I just didn't have the time to work on it!

Then on to the touch tone phone, I went. I got everything the ad in the phone book described as far as the receptionist was concerned. Visa and Mastercard accepted, we'll send someone over today if you'd like and what level of service do you want? Our man could be by before lunchtime, she told me, and he'll be spraying the lawn for pests, laying down weed killer, new seed, and fresh plant food. Weekly sessions would follow, yada, yada, yada. I went to my office upstairs and started in on the day's work, figuring my maintenance man would get here when he got here.

When he did, what a treat for sore eyes and dried brush. Maybe he wasn't the same man as in the ad...he was better! Even the protective gear couldn't hide this man's fantastic body.

"Hi! My name's Mike and I'm from Grass Roots Yard Services!" He offered me his hand and shook it with a grip strong enough to uproot a maple. "You're Mr. Borders?"

"Yes I am, and please call me Gene." And please don't look at the hard on that I'm getting, I thought to myself.

"Let's see then..." Mike squinted over an order form and read it back to me. "Full service level 3 for the back yard area, weed killer, new seed and plant food." He smiled up from the clipboard, an easy smile full of masculinity. "Show me the way and I'll get started."

Mike, Big Mike! Hot buzz cut, great moustache, goatee and solid as a rock, Mike! Covered in black rubber gear. I took him around back and showed him where the hose and spigots were hooked up, then I let him assess the plant life. He seemed satisfied that he wouldn't need any more help from me, so I excused myself and went upstairs to my office. Lucky for me, my desk window overlooks the entire yard. I had an unlimited view of Big Mike and whatever he was up to...and we both went straight to work.

I settled in behind my desk and loosened up my pants. Yeah, I could see Big Mike from my work table. If he tended all his yards looking like that, no wonder the plants grew so stoutly! I want him to give me a full service contact contract, man to man job. He can gladly give me new seed every week. Hell, I'd pay for it on a daily basis.

My mind started to wonder...out by the fence, in the dark shadows of my elder trees. He'd carve my bark and see the pink inside. He'll dump his fertilizer on me if he wants to. Yeah, I'll lie there and take it, let him put on a pair of heavy rubber protective gloves and smear it all over my sprouting chest. Let him show me how to keep a real man's garden in shape. Water it, hose it down until it sloshes with overflow. So much that he needs to use his boots to walk on it and stomp it firm. Yeah, he controls the growth, not me. Shape it, shave it, and trim it like a hedgerow.

If he doesn't like my progress or the way I follow his instructions, what then? Will he just leave me out in the sun, drying up, turning brown? Big Mike looks like he won't tolerate second rate service from anybody. A heedless disregard on my end would leave me crazy in the heat, begging for water, any water, my ass and balls getting insect bit. Twisting and turning while I plead for his attention, with him ignoring me until he thinks I'd suffered enough to have learned my lesson.

Then he's going to roll me into the mulch that lines the side of the house and turn my own hose against me. Long green rubber tube spraying water all over me, as I try to gulp down what I can catch. Ice cold water on my body where moments before was boiling hot sun and burning ant bites. Big Mike knowing all of these will make me squirm for his attentions, his control. He'll jam that black rubber boot into my chest and roll me in the mulch until I'm caked with it. Clods of dirt and chunks of bark clinging to my body, getting tangled in my hair and wedged in my crack, then a more personal hosing off, one that marks my ass as his own private tree trunk.

God damn! I'm sure glad he couldn't see me from here. Even in my air conditioned office I was hotter than hell, giving myself a personal weed whacking under my desk. If he'd spotted me then, it would've probably sent him back to tell his brother Rooters about the nut he just got through with. Big Mike must've been feeling the heat, too. He just took off his black rubber jacket and guzzled a drink from the hose. The water was running down that redwood sized chest of his and it poured off his Speedos. What I'd have given to plant myself between those rubber boots, face up, catching a cool drink as the water ran off his crotch!

If he wetted me enough, I'm sure my tree would grow. If I was really lucky, he'd be digging his root into me, too. Big Mike must not of thought anyone was watching, because he slipped the Speedos entirely, letting them go to the grass, over his boots and right down to the ground. I wanted to worship the high rubber as I watched Big Mike stretch out to the sun, water still glistening off his nearly naked body. He probably didn't mind if anyone might be watching, he looked so at ease with the outdoors. The strongest men are grounded by their boots, and as he arched his chest skyward and flexed his arms above his head, I knew that this man was a natural god. His glorious cock turned towards me, and I finally got to see my yard man in nature's full fantastic splendor.

This is when I wanted him, right there, when he could hold me down under the warmth of the summer sun. The smell of the freshly watered grass all around us, and the cold wetness of the ground against my chest. My pants off and away while Big Mike, this relaxed mountain of a man, taking me for a ride on his dick, his energies being transferred into me while my hands ripped and dug into the soil behind my house. Everything in me responding to the full-on sensual completeness of this man, so at home with his sexuality and the out doors, that's when he explodes at last inside me, it's like the center of the world is reaching up through my ass and into the magnetism of his dick.

My balls gave all at that point, smearing the under-wood of my desk with a coating of wood preserver no furniture company could market. Pressured spray pumping like a jet pack, and exhausting me as I overlook. I roared like a wildcat, too. That's what made Big Mike look up, Big Mike, his majestic body and boots, thick man-meat and steel body, cultivator of the finest order...catching me in the act of a mere peeping Tom. And he smiled at my window, winking, waving at me to come down.

I felt sheepish and stupid, yet as I approached him on the grass, Big Mike's smile never faltered. There was no contemptu- ous leering or mocking tone to his voice when he asked "Did you like my performance?"

Well of course I did, and I told him so. I also had to ask "Were you really just putting on a show or is that how you work for all your customers?"

"Hell, no. I knew what you wanted the second you showed me where the hose was. You can't hide a face like that. You want me to come by after work? I specialize in private care, and from the looks of things, your garage could use a load of fix-up."

Big Mike's Speedos were still on the grass, his boots were

still sparkling with water droplets. If he'd have asked, I'd have been lapping them clear in a heartbeat. Still not sure if I should follow this line of thinking, I figured it best to ask one more question. "You're a Lawn Maintenance man. Why talk about my garage and not my yard?"

Bending over to pick up his shorts and his jacket, he gave me another one of those casual looks that made me know sex this evening was a done deal. Big Mike flashed that confident smile and told me "Hey, I'll bring my boots. Indoors or outdoors, it doesn't matter to me."

"It grows where it grows."

EXIT ZERO

Along segments of the U.S. Interstate highway system, there are border crossings that fall within a specific nowhere land. A road that passes along a state line gets assigned a number to neither, or if it falls inside a mile of the state's border and first official exit. Appropriately enough, these passages are given an otherworldly designation: Exit 0.

There's a truck stop on the Texas/New Mexico border where I discovered something important about myself. The smell of diesel on asphalt and the sight of a leather boot made me want men. Not boys. They ran around the malls playing video games and wearing too much cologne. I saw myself like the men of the Exit Zero Diner. Sleeveless flannel shirts, muscles, body hair, greasy pants and especially the boots. Men unafraid of their own sweat, who felt no shame in flaunting a well packed basket. Confident enough to take a young boot-cub back into the big rig parking lot and show me the real deal about manhood.

The Exit Zero Diner was there before the safe-sex police put up concrete barriers to glory holes. It was easier for me then. All I had to do was turn my Cat Hat brim around, buckle up my boots and park myself in stall number two. Eventually I'd see something booted and brawny next door. From then on, I just had to trust my instincts.

It was on a Saturday afternoon that I decided, rather than hang around with the rest of the guys in my dorm, that I would wander down to Exit Zero and see where my boots would lead me. I browsed past the usual racks of chrome tire flaps and blue tinted lamp shields to the restrooms in the rear of the joint. I quickly cased the stalls, and seeing no tourists, took residence in my usual seat. And waited.

Not five minutes went by when stall number one got a customer. I could see them through the space between the cheap tile and institutional green metal of the stall. Engineer boots, black with aged creases and real big. Size fifteen triple-E no sweat. I heard the grunts and the flush and then...nothing. The size fifteens didn't straighten up. Whatever hunk of truck driving bruin was wearing them was relaxing in that stall, waiting. I was enough of a vet to know a cue when it presented itself. I popped my cock and balls through the graffiti sprawled wall, and right into a waiting, massive bear paw.

"Ummm. yeah, I just knew it," growled a horny voice from the other side. "There's always one here." His hand gave my shaft a sharp pull.

"Your boots, Sir," I stuttered in reply. "They're the biggest I've seen in a long time."

"Yeah, boy, you like them, you're gonna love my nips. In fact, I'm playing with 'em now. Balls too, boy. They hang bigger and lower than a Barrio Chevy." His hand continued massaging my dick.

"Please Sir, I'd love to lick them."

A low laugh from the other side. "Lick what, boy? My nips, my balls or my boots?"

"All of them, Sir."

My answer was rewarded with a real hard squeeze on my shaft. "I kind of like you where you are, faggot." I grimaced in silence as he resumed stroking me. "I bet if I play with this boy cock long enough, I'll get your jiz all over 'em." He waved his left foot under the stall crack just to fuck with me. "Then you'll really want to get that boy tongue of yours down on 'em."

That was enough to make my balls squirt up some pre-cum on the trucker's bare hand. "You ready to go for it, boy?" I felt a piece of rope go around my sac. "I'm having fun with my nips. I'm gonna shoot my load right here, right on my fuckin' super boots, get your load all over 'em too, boy." His voice was getting low and raw, I could tell he was close. So was I. His hand was moving faster on my shaft as the huge squared-off toes turned to face me in my stall. "Whaddya say, boy? You mess 'em up, you clean 'em off?"

"Yes Sir!" I couldn't contain myself anymore and my load flew out and across my neighbor's size fifteen triple-E's. He let out a series of grunts and, as I looked down, I could see the trails of spunk pooling on the insteps. His hand stayed tight on my dick.

"Still want to clean 'em off, boy?" came the gasping question. "if you do, you come out back and find the black cab with the orange panthers on the doors. I'll be here for another thirty minutes. If you can find me, you'll get your reward. I may even shoot another load on 'em for ya." He let go of my dick and the cum-covered boots stepped out of the stall, echoing towards the exit.

That's when I realized why he'd never let my dick drop. That asshole had stretched the string around my balls to the flush handle of the toilet! My balls were trapped against the wall until I either slipped out of the rope or someone found me. Lucky enough, in a couple of minutes my drained out balls just popped through the loop and I was able to back out from stall number two without any further humiliation. Mr. Fifteen Triple-E had obviously done this number on other guys before.

I hitched up my pants and turned the corner where the outdoor let on a field of semis. A black cab with orange panthers, huh? Well if Mr. Size Fifteen Triple-E wanted a challenge, this bootlicker was ready to prowl the entire Exit Zero Diner parking lot to beat it. The greatest problem was going to be getting past all those diesel distractions.

Like the two booted buddies sitting on the gate of a pick up truck. This tattooed bull of a man was explaining to his pal how he was going to get his prick tattooed next time he was in 'Frisco. All the while, he was sliding his foreskin around, showing his bud how the flames would stretch up the length from where his inner thighs, already framing his balls with an explosion of orange, to the head. His friend, who had taken his thick, uncut meat out as well, scratched at his balls and asked him all the usual "does it hurt" type of questions. But it wasn't the sight of the tattooed man's impressive chest and cock that mesmerized me. It was the boots. He had already unlaced them and was just letting them catch some air. His thick wool socks exploded over the tops, while the heavy leather tongue drooped, waiting for me to yank them off his feet. Saliva ran down my tongue, my re-hardening cock crept up my jeans. I imagined myself jamming my face down the shaft of the boot, pulling every last molecule of man-sweat into my nostrils before moving up to those burning orange tattooed thighs. Mr. Size Fifteen Triple-E had left my mind for the moment. I could only think of the intensity of the tattooed man's cum baptizing me, and how good that foreskin would taste. All the while, he and his bud casually talked about how hot that cock would look with some ink on it.

I was so immersed in my own fantasy that when a hand slipped over my mouth and spun me around, I didn't even hear him sneak up from behind. I was face to face with yet another brawny brute of a trucker, cigarette hanging from his lip and an epoch conveying a look of pure menace.

"Yell loud and lose yer teeth," he hissed. His hand slipped off my beard, but he wouldn't let my arm out from behind my back. "What are you staring at? You like those big dicks?" He pushed me against the front of his rig, heavy, greasy scent filling my head. His hand reached down to my crotch, squeezing my erection as a check. "Yeah, you want it. You might not get theirs, but sure as shit you're gonna get mine."

He put me on my knees, pulled his pants and jockeys away and a thick, smelly uncut slab flopped right in front of my nose.

I let the aroma of this cheese monster connect to my groin, letting my moustache brush against it, as his serpent began hardening. Closing my eyes, I took hold of the foreskin and slid it out, over my nostrils. Then I let my glance drop down to his steel tipped brown cowboy boots, spotted with oil and balls of asphalt, just waiting for an eager boot-slave tongue.

"How do you want it from me, boy?" He asked me as my mouth exploration began. I could only imagine this huge cock choking me as my slobber leaked over those filthy rodeo boots. He started pushing his hips into my face. "Which one of those dudes did you want more? The blondie or the one with all the ink?" He pulled my head away long enough to hear my answer. "The tattooed man, I wanted his boots."

This brought out a big snort of a laugh. "Have I got someone for you! Boots, huh? I'll get you fuckin' boots. Hey Snake! This punk says he wants boots!"

I had no idea who he was calling to, but I sure could hear him. As the evil man with the epoch kept on with his grinding cock, getting bigger and bigger with each thrust, a voice behind me rumbled pure southern thunder. "If he wants my boots, he's gonna have to earn thum. Right now he's wearin' too much shit. Dick, let him up fer chris' sakes. "

Dick let me up and I got my first look at Snake...and I knew I was in trouble. He made Dick and his epoch look like a choirboy who had skipped the showers for a couple of days. Snake was huge, with arching black eyebrows, wild black beard and a no bull-shit attitude. Wild tats were all over his rebel body, with rodeo bulls, flying skulls, rough riders and, on his back, a full color Confederate flag. A rattlesnake with fangs bared looped around his tight torso and stopped at his crotch, ready to snap at anything that got too close. He looked me up and down, took the cigar out from his beard and said, "You want some boots, I want some ass. Get naked!"

My shirt was first to go, but not fast enough for Snake and Dick. They ripped away anything left until I was bare assed naked in the parking lot of the Exit Zero Diner between the two of them. Snake started undoing his belt and asked Dick "How's he as a cocksucker?"

"Not bad."

"Ain't good enough! No one gets Snake's dick until he's great. You want my boots, boy? You go down on Dick's dick until he tells me you're fucking great. If he tells me you're not fucking great," he doubled his belt in his hand, "I'll give you some inspiration! Dick, let him at it."

Dick grabbed me by the hair, jamming his throbbing cock all the way down in one choking thrust. Before I could let my muscles relax, he grunted "just okay."

Whack! Wham! Snake's belt criss crossed my ass. The two of them continued this little scene for what seemed like eternity; I couldn't tell which side of heaven or hell I was on. The sounds and smells of the Exit Zero lot filled my head as a monster dick slammed down my throat, my ass cheeks burning from Snake's belt. And deep in my mind, the potential promise of this cigar smoking redneck's boots stayed in place.

My vertigo was interrupted by Dick, who was approaching his peak. "Gettin' better," he rasped.

A grunt from Snake, who, without warning, forced his rubber covered cock between my red hot ass cheeks. It felt like an ax handle! If my mouth hadn't been so thoroughly stuffed with prick, I'm sure any drowsing soul in his sleeper cab wouldn't have missed my screams of agony/ecstasy. Dick didn't even miss a beat, his shudders intensified as Snake started riding me from the other end. With a fearsome roar, Dick let out a shout of "Yeah, fuckin' great!" His cum exploded down my throat as Snake, with a guttural howl, let my burning ass fill with his fire of seed. I fell to the ground, and Snake stepped around, his boots in front of my gasping, exhausted face. "Fuckin' great, eh Dick?" Dick flashed a big ass smile as he pulled his pants back up and tucked away that fore skinned monster. "Well I think Snake's found himself a brand new boot boy. Get up, asshole."

Snake hoisted me off the ground and opened the door to a nearby rig. "Get in and behind the driver seat." He climbed in behind me and sat in his big leather seat and took off those socks and boots. "Put these socks over your hands and lie on your gut. Then put your hands over your head." I did as I was told, and he stuffed my sock-gloved hands into a pair of boots bolted onto the cab's wall. A tiny padlock secured the buckles on each, locking me in place and then he wedged a boot on either side of my head. Their odor overcame the cabin's combination of old fast food, cigars and sweat. Snake fired up another stogie and started up his rig. "Get real familiar with the smell of my boots, boy. I gotta haul this load all the way to the Carolinas and by the time we get there, I'm gonna want a boot-job real bad. If you ain't fuckin' great, well..." a low laugh of southern thunder rumbled through the cabin..."Snake's boots take a lickin' or I start kickin'."

With me in boot bondage and he a naked tattooed giant in the driver's seat, Snake pulled out from the lot of the Exit Zero Diner.

INNER TUBE

I want the inner tube.

It has been tethered to a pole in the stream. The cool water has flowed along its underbelly. The summer sun has made the upper half stretchy, soft. I want to take it out of the water and press that cool underside against my shorts. Take that hot, sun soaked top and squeeze it to my chest. The heat can flow into my nipples as the scent from the solar cooked rubber flows into my nostrils.

I fantasize where this inner tube has been. About the adventures it has likely witnessed. Maybe encased within the tough butyl shell of an eighteen wheeler's cab tire. I close my eyes and imagine how many miles this inner tube withstood of North American Interstates. Hot, burly truckers checking each other out at greasy spoons and showers, my inner tube parked on the hot, steamy asphalt of the truck stop. Absorbing the bumps of the pot-holes and the rocking cab while I pump the driver's ass at a rest area. All the while, that sun baked rubbery smell moves from my head to my crotch, thinking about how that big bear trucker sweat-ed on my cock while my inner tube accommodated the ride.

Maybe this inner tube pulled a farmer's plow through some soft, pliable soil. The mud splitting in half, just like his ass cheeks in the barn where I first met him. The musky smell of rubber tires, straw and livestock. I bind him face first to the huge wheel of a John Deere, making him kiss the tire while my greasy fist explores his fiery hole. He bites the tire, chews it, and whispers moans into it. His cum runs down that tire as my prostate massage takes him over the edge. The mud from the fields that clung to his service boots is smeared off the rim of the tire as he is spread eagled across. My inner tube knows the sensual sweat of my captured farmhand, as it hears his screams of pleasure.

I want to poke a tiny hole in this inner tube. As rich as the smell of the outside rubber is, I want to breathe in the stale air that has been confined within for who knows how long? Months? Years? All that heat and cold, making it expand and contract, accumulating into one incredible burst of aroma, better than any poppers. And it will make me higher than any drug. Do I need to tell any of you how spiritual and sexual that moment will be? The hiss of that air, my inner tube pressured to the near bursting point. Just like my balls, filled with the sacrament of this one rare opportunity. And all the air that has stayed under the protection of a luscious rubber temple, waiting for the freedom of my pen knife, like a genie in a flexible bottle.

I want to cut this inner tube in half. I know that it has supported the bodies of men, from the farmer in the barn to my truckin' fuck buddy's sleeper cab. To the swim suited vacationer who lazily floated downstream before abandoning my inner tube to the elements. He lays back in the sun, his ass taking in the current as the skin of his swimmer's body tanned in the glow of the early afternoon. The hot rubber smells following him to his destination. His hands splashing water on to it when it got too hot. Then searching the narrow zone below his swim suit crotch when the heat became too much for him there. Losing the suit when he decides no one will see him. Salmon aren't the only creatures releasing their sperm into the open water. I imagine a small white thread in the stream, following my inner tube through the hidden valleys between the wooded, secluded stream banks.

I take the separated halves of my inner tube, its air liberated and savored. I want to stick the serrated edges in my mouth and let my tongue roll across them. Spongy and soft, tasty and chewy. More so than any kind of gum. Did you know that chewing gum was first invented when explorers found natives chewing on sap from rubber trees? Fuck Wrigleys. I want Michelin. I want my spit on the real thing. I want the rubber from my inner tube in between my jaws, that's double my pleasure. That's what makes my Bazooka go off.

I want to find someone to wear my inner tube. Just like a perfect cocoon, one half up over his legs, pinning them together. The second piece over his shoulders, trapping his arms at his sides. A long, black seal, leaving him lying there with only his feet, head, cock, balls and ass free to play with. As I wish to play with. He stretches against the walls of his rubber trap, so thin, so flexible, yet so unrelenting. He can push against it all he wants, but I am his Rubber Master. All I have to do is rub my hands against the inner tube, and he will feel it echo along the length of his body. He becomes harder as my caresses stroke the rubber... there is no need to touch his skin. He has a new skin now. I could put a latex hood over his head, so all he will see is the black...all he will smell is the rubber.

I want to wear my inner tube. I can take my pen knife and cut away the old valve stem. I lie back on the ground and slide inside the rubber, my own sweat providing me with all the lubricant I need. That hole where I took away the sharp stem now has a new stiff object pointing through. I pop the balls out, one nut at a time. The other half of my inner tube pulls over my head, over my chest, confining my nipples. All I need to do is slap them, and my chest reverberates like a drum skin. Drag my palms across the most taught areas and the droning sound and glorious feel of rubber fills the stream bank. I have extended a percussion instrument across my body, all the while, taking in a soft sensual range against the contours of my body. My cock springs to life, now that my inner tube provides me with all the basic needs. The smell, taste, sound and…Yes, oh God, yes, the sensation of touch.

I take my rubber gloves and spit into them, going to work on my well loaded cock and balls.

I have my inner tube, it has me. It's time to baptize it.

SEWER RATS

My Mama once told me the story that I was late coming home from school. My pants were soaked all the way up to the belt, and my shoes were sopping and filthy. When she asked me why I was so wet, I told her that I had to stop and jump in every curbside puddle on my walk home. Like any good parent, the next question was why I would want to do such a thing. To which I replied...because it was fun. I guess I haven't changed all that much. I still want to put on high black rubber boots and stomp around in the mud.

Since maturing a bit, mud isn't all I want to force my feet in any more. It doesn't stop at the lower extremities, either. I want to find the thickest, soupiest mix and lower myself into tanks filled with it. I want to Gear up and then descend a ladder from a man-hole into the recesses of the city's waste disposal system. There's not a thing in the world finer than when my hardhat's headlamp dims from a spray of unexpected sludge from above.

Me and my buddies? We're Sewer Rats.

The darkness is our lifeblood. I realized that I wouldn't be happy in life unless I found a career that matched both my capabil-ities with my desires. My desires were the feel of rubber, sensa-tions of sludge, and the all-encompassing depths that little, if any light, can penetrate. To lose yourself underneath the frenetic sur-face world, getting lost in an underground space of smells, liquids, and naturally, sex. That's why I began studying bio-engineering and architecture. It gave me the access I needed to the city's infrastructure and nether world. As my studies continued, so did my interaction with others involved in the small world of the Department Of Water And Power's elite corps of sewer workers.

It didn't take long to find out that I was part of a like minded group of guys. These men, all seniors, felt a special affinity for the maze of tunnels that fed the city's drainage network. I was also amazed that they were all lovers of Rubber Gear! It was one of those things I just assumed was my own private fascination. That misconception was laid to waste by Tom, the foreman of my first crew, who took me aside to warn me about why he requested me for his work force.

"I've been watching you," he told me. "And I'll tell you now that my detail plays just as rough as it works. If you don't understand what I'm telling you, say so now. I'll get you in another fucking sissy crew."

I knew exactly what he was talking about. It scared me more than a little. Tom was no striped-suit. He had a beer-belly along with a blue collar attitude to match. There was plenty of muscle to back up any statement he made, and with thirty-five years with DWP, could tell you each and every intersection at all levels of the underground. His tenure at the DWP was legendary, as were his massive tattooed arms. Although it was also the stuff of legend, rumors of his sexual background and affinity for kinkiness ran through the ranks. More than a few leering comments were thrown in my direction when the announcement was made that Tom specifically wanted me for his crew.

"Just watch your ass." One particular co-worker warned me. "Because if he wants it, he won't take no for an answer. If he wants to lose you in the underground, he can do it, and it'll take you weeks to figure a way back up...if you do at all."

That wasn't a problem. I kept in shape during my studies, so my hip boots and waders fit me more than a little tight. I kept my body shaved so that my rubber tops clung. The hair on my head was clipped short so there was nothing for a gas mask or hood to get stuck on. I wanted to show these men that I wasn't only able to keep up with them for knowledge of the city's network of tunnels, but also through the physical exertion of pulling heavy equipment around these tunnels filled with drainage and shit. Hell, I wanted to be down there and I wanted to impress Tom's men. And more than a few times I had stroked my thick, uncut meat to the thought of Tom, with those ham sized arms of his, pinning me down and getting after my protective gear.

His chance didn't come as quickly as I figured it would. The other men on our team, all veterans, weren't hesitant about commenting about "Tom's new meat" or about "The new basket" I was packing. It was all too obvious...I was going to get a proper initiation with these horny bastards. I looked forward to it with a mix of heat and nerves. How rough was the "play" Tom was talking about?

The first couple of details were uneventful with Tom, and his men being little more than a bunch of fanny slapping brothers in a workers' corp. I was thinking that my lust might have been a product of my hyperactive imagination and the DWP rumor mill. That didn't stop me from sporting a constant hard-on underneath my chest high rubber leggings and tightly confining gas mask and jacket. There was also plenty of rank sewage to satisfy my desire for sludge. It wasn't until a couple of weeks later that Tom made his move.

"Randall" he bellowed "level seven today." He still hadn't given in to calling me anything else but Randall, even though the rest of the crew had started calling me Red in honor of my brassy close-cropped hair. Level seven was a tricky area, one of the oldest, and out of all the city tunnels it was the most labyrinth like. We were to investigate a drainage block that was reported to be backing up the main drainage line into Sector 2120's sewage treatment center. This was going to be a tough day, and no pun intended, a real shit of a detail. Lots of gear, lots of sludge, and a load of work. I could already feel my dick getting hard. I suspected nothing more than an enjoyable day on the job.

We loaded up a truck and one other man, a tall lanky DWP man named Sam came with us. Level seven duties were restricted to three men at a time, a triple-buddy system meant to keep the extremely close quarters of the ancient tunnels workable. More than three people down there would make moving around next to impossible. Sam was such a scrawny fuck that his maneuvering in those tubes wouldn't be a problem at all, and 18 years in Tom's crew made him one of the most experienced of the Sewer Rats.

Once we got downtown and found our entry hole, we rigged our surface radio for Jack, our street side man. Tom went down the ladder first. I adjusted my gas mask and followed, taking in my day's first rubber filled breath of underworld dankness. Sam slid down the ladder after us, his gear in tow and his headlamp already blindingly on. Tom led us with his unerring sense of direction, around trenches and piping, through grates and down ladders, into more narrow older tunnels, leaving directional markers at any point that our paths changed. We made it to the brink of our level seven entry point, where the blockage was reported to be. We had to undo a grating that kept us from delving into an area that only the four legged rats knew better than Tom, and he cackled over his radio that Sam was going through this one first.

"If there really is that much shit in there," he wise-cracked, "your skinny ass is the only one that will fit through."

Sam slipped easily into the slimy, algae covered duct that led to our final destination. When he radioed back that everything was ready, Tom followed. Then he called back for me, telling me to haul my ass through the tunnel. I pushed my hip boots into the opening and moved sideways into the hole...only to feel something take hold and pull me roughly through.

This was Tom's little trick...there was only a distance of about four feet between this slime filled pipe and the next space! Sam and Tom, as soon as they saw my ankles appearing on the other side, had slipped a coil of rubber tubing around my feet like a lasso and snared me like a doomed rodent. I was yanked into a very large, dimly lit space, almost like an abandoned cavern. My wrists were pulled over my head and I was lifted into a standing position, and Sam quickly switched off my helmet radio before any protests could be broadcast back to Jack on street side. I had been successfully ambushed by my foreman and his second in command, trapped seven levels below the city, where the air was so dank that moss hung from the walls in strings and cords. We were down so deep, that I had no idea where we were.

"Welcome to my private workshop, asshole" Tom shouted into my ear.

As my eyes became more accustomed to the dim light, I could see just what he meant. There were metal crosses against the walls, block and tackles suspended from the high ceiling, a sling off to one corner, and several tables that were obviously meant for restraining devices. There were also some very old looking chests along the walls, all looking very airtight and covered with the mossy growth that dominated this level of subterranean ductwork. Sam took a hook from one of blocks and pulled me into a position where my boots barely touched the ground, and Tom gave my wader enclosed nuts a good squeeze.

"Today's assignment, Randall? No records, no papers. The crew knows where we are, they just don't really know where 'here' is. Sam is the only one who has ever been in my space more than once. There's no record of this station in the City's files. I could keep you down here for as long as I want, and no-one would know where to look." He put one of those big arms around me and clutched my ass hard. "So you just do what Mr. Boss Man tells you to, and you'll pick up a paycheck on Friday. Got that, boy?" This time it was Sam that slapped my ass hard!

"Yes Sir!" I shouted from behind my mask. "Good boy," Tom replied, going over to one of the cabinets and undoing it with one of his many keys. I could see him removing several articles, but there just wasn't enough light to tell what they were. I watched as Sam went over to a huge fly wheel and began turning it. His wiry, rubber suited body showed every sinew as he pushed the valve with all his strength. Tom came back over to me, carrying several coils of rubber hoses and tubing. "Ever cum in a tank, boy?"

The tubes began to snake their way around my knees and hips, as Tom began designing an elaborate rubber harness around my body. I could only twist in whatever direction my foreman aimed me, with rubber stretching around my crotch and balls, cinching my basket tight. I still couldn't tell what Sam was doing with those pipe valves, but Tom's comment gave me a good guess.

My jacket was undone so that my skin was open to Tom's gloves and his rubber clad fingers. I could hardly see his face through the lenses, but I sensed he was taking a fair amount of amusement from my plight. He pulled at my tits and pinched my nipples repeatedly, playing my upper body to full effect. He wrapped more tubing around my chest, then over and around my shoulders. Sam joined him as they lifted me off the block. My hands were undone, but only briefly. While Sam held me to the damp cement floor, Tom bound my wrists before my chest, linking the tubing to the harness already in place. My elbows were secured to the knotted rubber at my sides. I was totally helpless before these two demanding sewer rats, seven levels below the city streets; in a cavern that no-one knew.

Tom undid his rubber pants' zipper seal, and an erect, red cock appeared in front of my mask. He pushed it inside my open jacket, rubbing it roughly against my sore nipples. "You had your chance, Randall. I told you I like to play hard. You stayed on my crew." He laughed like a bear in heat. "Now you're going to learn why everyone calls me Sir." I felt a trickle of wet warmth, then more, increasing into a torrent of piss down the inside of my shirt and running inside of my waders. It seemed to never end...this soaking. "And if I'm not around, you listen to my man Sam!"

Another block and tackle went over my shoulders, as Sam came around in front of me. "You got a hot ass, boy," he told me. Smack! "And if I want to, I get to pound on it." Smack! Again a hard blow through the tubes and rubber pants. Then Tom and Sam pulled on the ropes and lifted me off the ground to guide my immobilized body along a track in the ceiling. As I twisted in mid-air along side of my fiendish co-workers, I finally got to see what Sam was doing when he was spinning the valve wheel. Below me, on either side, was a pair of deep metal tanks, filled with ooze. I couldn't tell what was in the first, but the second took no guess-work at all.

It was a vat of unprocessed sewage, thick, dark, bits of tissue visible on the surface. Lumps were floating around the tank's edge. The smell, even through my mask, was overwhelm-ing. Even in my bondage and anxiety, my dick began to leak pre-cum. I knew what my foreman and his sadistic accomplice were thinking of.

Tom reached at my crotch and grabbed onto my tent pole. "Yeah, you fucking rat, you want to swim in that shit pool, don't you, boy?" I could barely nod in my confinement. Pulling my rubber restrained cock like a handle, he positioned me aside the other vat of sludge, the one that was not immediately identifiable. "This room used to be a sump station" Tom began. "It was pretty busted up twenty five years ago, but I started repairing. Then I found out that there wasn't a record of the place, and it'd been listed as closed the year I started working for the city. I put my tools and toys down here, and then I showed Sam where it was after the first time I tied his skinny ass up...just like you are now." Smack! Sam took another well aimed blow at my ass.

"I see you can tell that it's shit in that tub. That's for dessert, boy." Tom let my rock solid dick go, much to my relief. That left me slowly twirling next to the slick looking grunge in the first vat. He and Sam pulled me up a few more feet, and then shifted me till I was centered over the foul smelling liquid.

"The sumps work fine now." Tom's rubber jacketed arms grabbed my boots and held me still." I can collect up as much of the city's shit as I need, anytime I want to haul some suit's nose over their dick. You'd be amazed how many fucking suits have been right where you are now boy...but they beg like little pussies." Both Sam and Tom shared an evil laugh at some wicked memory. "Yeah, I get a good salary, and I can work for as long as I need to. These fucking suits...scared of getting their shoes dipped in a little bit of shit. Makes 'em wet their undies and promise you anything. Not you, boy! You just can't wait to feel this seeping into your boots, can yah, boy?"

He let the rope on the block and tackle out just a short ways, and my feet slipped below the surface of the liquid. I still didn't know what it was in that vat. Tom took a glove full and smeared it allover the tops of my rubber bound boots. My dick squirted another pulse of pre-cum against my restraints. "It's drainage from the refinery sector," Tom chuckled. "Water, oil, grease, all collected into a special tank for recycling. I just borrow some every once in a while. Nice and thick, slimy as hell! Just wait until Sam rubs your dick with it." Another couple of inches, as my shins start disappearing. Sam dipped his fingers in it and drew four greasy lines, war-paint style, across his face.

"That's seven feet of the finest used crank case grease and motor oil you'll find in this city. My tubs sink into the floor two feet from the base and come up five feet...deep enough to sink a blubbering suit if he thinks I don't mean it when I tell him he don't mess with me or any of my men. Understand, boy?" Another slip on my rope; my knees now immersed in the oil. My feet are getting warm from the liquid's thickness; my dick continues twitching in the excitement of my rubber imprisonment. I can only picture some bound and gagged executive trying like hell to keep his legs out of this oil...when I on the other hand want to beg Tom to sink me in all the way.

"Yeah, boy...hard as a rock, you go into this tank, you're all mine and you'll be taken care of." More rope off the block, I sink just below my waist. Tom's piss still washes inside my pants; my dick is just above the surface. I grunt behind my mask. Sam leers and dips his glove in. He lets it drip oil right in front of my crotch. I feel my hips thrust at those distant fingers, which might as well be in Iowa for all I can do about it. "Go ahead Sam...he wants it bad enough, give him some. But boy, you cum now and you don't get seconds."

Sam slips his hand under my waders and lets his fist stroke my dick with the greasy liquid. It's almost more than I can take, and Sam pulls his hand out just as fast as he stuck it in. Tom lets a big section of rope out and I'm up to my tits in glorious oil. God, it feels fantastic. Bubbles are popping up at the surface just below my face, as air caught inside my waders starts releasing. My shirt and leggings give way to the slow tantalizing ooze of thick motor oil. My mask protects me from the toxicity, but permits me the luxury of inhaling the heady brew. Tendrils of cool rich slime fill every space between my rubbers and my body.

"Whose team do you work for, boy?"

"Yours, Sir!"

"And who do you take orders from?"

"You Sir!"

"If I'm not here?"

"Sam, Sir!"

"Damn straight, boy."

Tom and Sam grab the rope and began the laborious task of lifting my grease soaked rubber body out from the grunge vat. My hips felt like a loose grenade, I wanted to cum so bad. But my captors had more in store for me. Once they had given me a few minutes to drip off a bit, Tom took a piece of pipe and pushed me over the tub of sewage. I was again, centered right above it, and there was just no way to stop my torment now. I was too far gone; I would do anything this big, bad demanding boss wanted. He knew it, too. I could tell by his laughter.

"You a Sewer Rat, boy? Ready to say 'Fuck off to any suit who tells you to nark on me and my men?"

"Yes Sir!" I shouted; writhing so badly that I was wondering what would happen if the rope holding me in the air would snap. Tom didn't tease this time, though. He and Sam let down the rope with no break, and I plunged into the foul mix like a fish to water. The cesspool-cocktail filled in the space where the grease was, and I could see the oil coming to the watery surface around my shoulders. What happened next, though, surprised me. I had almost forgotten the monstrous dick Tom had pulled out when he first warmed me up with his precious piss. He and Sam climbed on to the edge of the vat, Sam also with his dick out of his rubber pants. It matched his body perfectly, long, wiry and hard as steel.

"Let's see some white on all that brown, Sam." The two of them began stroking each other with their well lubricated rubber gloves, while I dangled, immersed in raw shit. My own useless hands were unable to touch my roaring hard-on, but that wasn't going to matter much longer. Seeing these two men, my rubber-ized foreman and his lieutenant jacking off while my bound in rub-ber crotch felt the sloshing of oil and shit inside my gear would do it. With an animal grunt, Sam came first, and then with a shout to match his girth, Tom shot his load. Cords of white fell across my mask and that last bit of incentive tripped my trigger...my spunk fired into my rubberized, lubricated confinement as I gave in with a heavy shudder.

"Good thing he's got his mask on, eh Sam," Tom leered at me. "Wouldn't want to get any of that cum in his pretty red hair. Ain't that right, Randall boy? You did put your mask on good and tight, didn't ya?" I nodded weakly. "Good boy then. Hold your breath, pig."

At that moment, he let out the remains of the rope and my hooded head slipped under the surface of the tank. I thrashed in a panic for only a moment, the sudden fear that maybe he meant to leave me here where no-one would know...then popping back up over the surface of the shit-pool as Sam and Tom pulled me over the edge of the tank. Still bound and harnessed, I was hoisted over the wall, above a huge storm drain, as my exhausted body dripped cum, sludge, shit, piss and sweat into the city's drainage system.

I couldn't see Sam; he had once more disappeared from view. Tom was right in front of me. "That's right, Randall boy. You're a real Sewer Rat now...one of Tom's boys. You don't take shit from nobody."

And that's when Sam turned the fire hose on me.

VANILLA EXTRACT

"Heh, heh HEH, heh heh heh!"

Pardon me, I was just practicing. Once, I recall Stephen King writing that any true personification of madness must have a distinctive laugh. "Danse Macabre," I believe. It's just that I don't think King had the same concept of Dungeons that I do. Yes, I am a Leather-man, a practitioner of S&M. Sexual Magic, if I may. By virtue of your reading this, I'll assume you are, too.

If I could reach you, I would hurt you. Not just in any specifically pain filled way, just one that you would enjoy in a manner that would linger for a while. A gentle caress with my cat or a quick sharp shock with my wand, enough to titillate you, make you beg your Master for more. Unfortunately for you, even if I had you within my reach, there wouldn't be much I could do to assuage your hungers.

Because I've gone mad!

My playroom, my elaborate gorgeous dungeon, looks different of late. The enema bags are dangling full, but not with warm soapy water. The tens unit has been running constantly, yet the leads are not attached to a freshly shaved scrotum. You see, gentle reader, I've finally decided that these long lonely evenings of rare tricks and one handed reading had to cease. My looks, through the molding ways of time, may be distinguishing me to the semblance of a Master Daddy; still, I am not getting any younger. Even with degrees in Biochemistry, Electrical Physics and Molecular Theory, I alone can't turn back calendars. So it is time for revenge, to take those long collected skills as a brilliant Top, a best boy submissive, an academic genius and use them to my advantage.

See that long black case positioned between the racks of dildos? You think it is a cock sheath, perhaps? Maybe a vibrator?

No, foolish voyeur! It's a reconstructed laser sight that I've modified a bit. Those rubber restraints make excellent supports, ceramic ass-eggs now insulators. The piss gag holds it level and the hand crank generator provides the power peaks.

It's not a dungeon anymore. It's a laboratory. Both have remained equally secret from the masses. The only parts that haven't been realigned for my less than obvious purposes have been the prison cell and the mock electric chair...where a pretty military hair cut now prickles with the static in the air. His blue eyes flash above the red ball gag I playfully rolled into his mouth. When I tweaked his well expanded nipple at the Fault Line last night to test him, he smiled and bowed his head, just like a good submissive. When he pressed his face into my jacket with just a hint of a whimper, I asked him what he would do for surrender.

"Anything, Sir," my little puppy responded. Would he accept electrical play?

"Yes Sir, gratefully." Such a good boy. And if I secured him in my cell, would he writhe and moan for my pleasures, knowing all too well that it would excite me and force me to advance his limits beyond his wildest imagination?

"Yes Sir. Please Sir, take me with you and shock me till I scream my thanks."

Delightful young man, to bad he couldn't know the wild gyrations of my mind. Electrical shock was not what I had in mind for my little lab rat. More like sugar shock.

Now my handsome young blonde thing looks at me through those baby blues with genuine fear, because what is about to happen to him is a scene beyond what he thought he'd be as we parted the cigar smoke of the bar and rode my motorcycle back deep into the North Hollywood flats. You see, all the modifications to my dungeon have transformed it from being Southern California's most elaborate playroom into a science lab of unequaled capabilities. All those toys, now worked into the tools of molecular reconstruction. Those computers, once used for the connection to tricks via BBS and modem, now combine atomic puzzles with lightening fast accuracy. The cookbook my gorgeous lab rat saw when I pulled his naked, chained body from the cell to the electrical chair is open to the cupcake section. As I fastened the belts around his chest and neck, made certain that his ankles and wrists wouldn't flail about, I watched as his eyes darted across the recipes, somewhat confusing him. Unknown to the boy, he was seated before a matter recombinant ray, a tightly refined beam that will restructure the molecules of human flesh and bone into fructose, sugar, assorted dairy products and preservatives. Instead of idling away the hours bemoaning the utter lack of real, committed slaves available for me to torture to orgasm, I've invented a particle laser that will transform human beings into junk food.

Life is like a box of pastries...Yum!

Sure my squirming little test subject got played with last night. Even an insane genius keeps his promises. There's plenty of Crisco inside his well stretched asshole. He took it by the handful, the grateful piglet. Saran wrap glistens with sweat around his chest, waist, cock and balls. Mean Master that I am, not a drop of his creamy cum has yet to be wasted on the floor of my playroom. After all, what's a cupcake without a frosting center to bite down on? He only struggled when I slid the baking tin under his ample butt.

Now my laser sighting darts from nipple to nipple, my naked subject grunting a gagged "mrrphhh" as he twists away from the tiny red dot that alarms him so. The generators are humming loud and clean, the needles on the tens unit are moving closer to the amperage I desire, coolant flows from the suspended enema bags, and I feel the tingle in that familiar spot beneath my lab coat.

SNAP!

In one blinding flash, followed by patterns of green light dancing around my facsimile of an electrical chair, in the center of the baking pan I placed under a sexy, firm ass, sits a large yellow cupcake surrounded by plastic wrap.

My first attempt at changing the dietary habits across the Gay Ghettos of America is a success. That's one less trick I have to take into WeHo for breakfast...

*   *   *   *   *

Heh, heh HEH, heh heh heh.

Yes, it is me again. I've put on some weight since you've last heard from me. After all, I had to do something with all my little science projects. But you, laughing behind the anonymous screen of your computer, you'd better watch your boots. Right now you look like an éclair to me.

I've been doing a lot of thinking lately. Those Tops and bottoms that I have taken on a one way trip to Jenny Craig; Hell just aren't getting me off the way they did after my first... ahem... taste of success. Their struggles in the cell were so delicious. The roar of disbelief as I smear cooking grease along their engorged desperate to explode cocks or pour hot, waxy chocolate across their breasts as they squirm mightily. The discovery that the fur on a hairy chested bear turns into a delectable likeness of toasted coconut. Just for fun, I stuffed maraschinos in the mouth of one subject, because I wanted to see if it was possible to get your cherry back.

But one or two pitiful pastries a week isn't doing it. So my dungeon lab has been the site of some down-sizing experiments. Thus, on my old physician's table lies the fruits of my labor...my particle beam in a compact, portable form. When I asked my regular mechanic to install additional batteries in the back of my car, he thought it would be used for one of those impossibly loud automotive stereo systems, he chided me for adding to Hollywood's noise pollution.

Yes, very funny, I told him. Heh, heh HEH, heh heh heh. Not bad for a future Ding Dong.

Vanilla Extract

Even now, I've discovered variations on my humble invention. With a few minor modulations on molecular intensity, I've been able to concoct a combination of products on my particle laser. There are now three major settings; one for creampuff, one for cupcake, and another, which I've ironically decided to label...heh heh... twinkie.

None of which matters, of course without a road test. Seeing how you've made the journey with me thus far, then our minds will have probably reached the same conclusion as to where the greatest collection of pound cake could be found. Forthwith, we are off to West Hollywood, and Santa Monica Boulevard in our first cruise.

Those biting battery cables dig into the lead of my new toy's power source, as my jeep engine idles along towards the Astro Burger, the scene of the afternoon's first experiment. Putting by, the meters reading accurately, and with one little twitch on my trigger...

SNAP!

...there's a creampuff sharing counter space with the jalapeno peppers. This is going to be a glorious little drive.

My jeep is leaving a trail of mayhem and sugar deposits along the strip. It makes me wonder, when I see a butch German Sheppard wolf down a curbside cupcake, if its female leash holder would shriek if she knew just what went down her bitch's gullet. My car seat can barely contain my excitement as my revenge continues. The front patio of the French Quarter; It's a desert buffet now. Circus Books' front entry; Reams of banana cream. Yet there is one little trick I dare to try, as my vehicle approaches a downtown disco. One broad sweep of the crowd, my ray set on twinkie, oh the irony of it...heh heh HEH!

I inch my jeep a little closer, get a knot of sweater clad blondies in my sight. My stomach flutters, my scrotum tightens, my settings register as I start the sequence...

But what? They aren't even twitching! My meters, rising above their red points, the car batteries cracking...oh dear Einstein, it's molecular feedback from my own invention, it can't make the distinction...I've set it for twinkies, it thinks it's hitting twinkies...my fabulous easy-bake weapon, before my eyes...it melts into a sticky, spent, doughy mass of inert putty. Who would've imagined that a cordon of twinkies would save West Hollywood from my special brand of evil?

I writhe, I contort, I howl at the mountains of the valley. But not for long.

You see, gentle reader, while working out the details of miniaturization, I came across a slight variation on my original plan for molecular reconstruction, one that has enormous potential.

A particle beam that will transform leather and spandex into whale blubber.

Heh heh HEH, heh heh heh.

CHROME

His coffee was cold. Not that it mattered to him anymore.
The waitress would come by and refill it, just as she had for the
past four hours. He'd taste it again and then hold the cup for a
while longer. The mug was nothing more than a prop to occupy
his time, and right now, he had plenty of that. The notebook on
the table was open, and in front of him, in large black letters, was
written "San Antonio?" It was more of a plea than a question. So
far, it was a plea that had been ignored.

Thus had Alan Gallagher's highway to hell week been so
far. For the second time since trying to return from California to
Texas, his car had broken down and left him stranded at a desert
truck stop, in the middle of nowhere, watching as night fell and his
funds continued to run out. But this breakdown was for keeps.
Alan knew that sound, the automotive equivalent of a Hollywood
Death Scene, and was positive this time his old car had given up
the road ghost and blown its engine. The steam and oil smoke,
the ugly pool of black scum under the engine, the bang bang
BANG of a seizing motor as his trusty mini wagon crunched its last
inch of asphalt along the berm of New Mexico Interstate Ten.
Then to top it all off, a scorpion road kill outside the driver's side
door as Alan stepped out to at least give a perfunctory glance
under the hood.

"Talk about bad omens," he muttered to himself, retrieving
his lone suitcase and briefcase. Alan also remembered that after
twilight, scorpions and snakes tended to come up to the still warm
asphalt. He decided that if the sun was going to set on him before
he got a ride, he'd better stay close to something off ground zero.
As luck would have it, someone did stop, and were at least willing
to carry him into the next town. That's where Alan was now, sitting
alone with his fourth hour of coffee, his notebook begging some

east bound trucker for a lift. It had already gone dark when a large greasy hand landed on the table, covering the entire page of Alan's written plea.

"San Antonio, huh. I could get you to El Paso and you could catch a Greyhound from there." Alan looked up to see what kind of giant could blanket his paper with just his palm. One big, square jawed trucker stood over him, bent at the waist with his arms planted on the diner's table. Those hands could've encompassed Alan's coffee mug and still had room to spare. A solid black line linked his eyebrows and his upper lip was covered with an extra inch of protruding moustache. "What are you doing here, and why you going to San Antonio?"

Alan began the long saga about moving to Texas, going back to LA to retrieve his old car, and how each day since had been weirder and more frustrating, leading up to that day's kamikaze engine dismount. "That about sums it up," he said with half a smile. "I think it's God's way of telling me I'm not supposed to move to Texas. Even my car threw in the towel rather than cross the border."

What Alan got next from the trucker threw him for a loop. There was a roaring blast of laughter as the big man sat down across from him and said, "I saw your car about twenty-five miles back. Liked the stickers, too."

Alan knew what he meant immediately, he had placed in the lower corner of the rear window, a Leather Pride Flag sticker several years ago. Before that, a friend of his had surprised him by applying a rainbow sticker on the bumper. Anyone with the knowledge could figure out what kind of man was driving that car. Alan stuck his hand out to the giant across the diner table and introduced himself. "I'm Alan Gallagher."

The big man took Alan's hand in a handshake that was as warmhearted as it was solid. "Name's Rich Wharf... but everyone calls me Wolf." Alan didn't have to ask why. Nor did he have to think very hard when Wolf told him "We don't see many men like you around here. Can I buy you some dinner so we can talk?"

Chrome

Wolf was an independent trucker who had retired on disability a few years ago. An accident had left both knees injured and because of his size, made any kind of work involving more than a couple of hours legwork near impossible. Even accelerators, brakes and clutches were off limits now, but as he explained to Alan, short hops of a few hundred miles were okay and taking money under the table didn't bother most of the people he drove for. Tomorrow's trip to El Paso was less than six hours in his truck, and a couple hundred bucks here and there along with his savings kept him going just fine. As he took on a hungry look to his eye, Wolf added, "It makes it easier for me to build new toys for the barn. Now about your car..."

"Yes?" Alan suspected that this is when the pride sticker question was going to come. The big man surprised him again.

"My old man owns New Mexico's oldest parts yard. He's also the man the States call to haul in abandoned cars. I'll give ya about twenty four hours before they call him after yours. If y'all want me to, I'll give you fifty for it, and that'll save ya the towing and impound fees. Plus I'll take ya to El Paso tomorrow and put ya on the first bus for San Antonio. I'll even put ya up for the night. Fair deal?"

Alan gulped hard. This man already knew what the stickers represented, and was now offering him an overnight place to stay. The leather jacket he'd been wearing all this time was suddenly very conspicuous, as well. How much of an ulterior motive did Wolf have here? "You liked the stickers, right?"

"Betcha I did." That look came back into Wolf's eyes. "And like I said, not many men like y'all stop in these parts. I'd sure love to show ya why my favorite color is chrome."

Even with his desire obviously showing, there was an openness to this man that Alan trusted. On instinct, he stuck his hand out again and said "You got yourself a deal."

Wolf gave him a big arm pump in return and laughed. "C'mon Cowboy. The truck's outside." He picked up Alan's suitcase and left payment for dinner on the table. Alan could only marvel that his suitcase looked proportionately like his briefcase next to this mountain in bib overalls. They pulled out of the truck stop lot and headed east on I-10.

There was a considerable stretch of mileage before they finally arrived at Wolfs place. It was a large old farm house next to an arch roofed barn, with a couple of rusted trucks parked off to the side and a rig pulled close to the front porch. The kind of place that Alan had fantasized about when truckers and bears in their natural habitat flowed through his mind. There was nothing frilly or pretentious about the house at all, and when Wolf asked Alan if he wanted some coffee, it was a gas stove in the comer of the kitchen as opposed to an electric one. There didn't seem to be much around by way of modern appliances, not even as much as a microwave. The only nod to the decade's parade of electronic toys were a small computer and a TV/VCR combo.

"You keep things pretty simple here, don't you?" Alan watched the steam rise off his coffee mug, the first one today that he actually felt like drinking from.

"I have two hobbies," replied Wolf. "Trucks and the barn, everything else is stuff I need to get by. C'mere." Alan got up from the table and went over to where the big man was sitting. When Wolf slapped his knee, Alan sat. "It's like I told ya, we don't get many men like y'all around here." Wolf began to breathe hard around Alan's neck. "Once in a while someone surfing the computer will stop by for a visit, but not too often. I tend to scare 'em off," he continued with a chuckle, "cause I got a real evil imagination."

I wonder how evil, thought Alan, even as his dick began pressing against the inside of his jeans. He felt Wolf's massive bone tough arm pinning him against his chest, almost like a boa constrictor's press. The tingle of the moustache and the heat of the big man's breath hardly made the pressure feel like a deadly crush. But, thought Alan, aren't snakes supposed to be able to hypnotize their prey before the final twist? Just to test the idea, he wriggled a bit under the lock of Wolf's arm, and Wolf reflexively squeezed him harder against his body. Alan liked this reaction; it made him squirm in reciprocation. Wolf was just whispering in his ear now, talking about the time he'd spent designing and adding inventions to the barn. Even the tiny reactive squirm brought a reaction from the big man. Wolf brought his other arm up over Alan's shoulder, pressing his head against Wolf's neck and chin, trapping his ear next to Wolf's mouth as the words become more tantalizing and the tangle of muscle and sentences became more inescapable.

Wolf's tongue began lapping at Alan's earlobe. "Y'all ready to play with a hungry Wolf?"

"Yes Sir."

"That's good. Just want to warn ya about a couple of things first. When we go out to my barn, when I shut and bar the door, we don't leave until after I ask you if you're ready to go. I already said that I got an evil imagination, so I want chya to know that this ride might get pretty damn scary. Understand?"

Alan nodded.

"Good. The other things to remember are I love control and I love chrome. Keep all that in mind, and the Wolfman will give a trip like your California buddies never even dreamed about."

The hard-on in Alan's pants got even more rigid and he gasped as Wolf loosened his grip in order to flip him across his shoulder. Wolf gave him a solid slap on the backside as he carried him across the front porch and out the driveway. "Get ready, cowboy. We're going in."

Wolf entered the barn and set Alan on his feet. A light came on and Alan got his first look at what he expected would be a dungeon beyond his wildest expectations. Instead, he was given the disappointing vision of automotive repair shop. There was a pickup with its hood up, a tray of tools out on a busted-up bedroom bureau and a red metal tool chest. About the only thing that looked threatening was the block and tackle with a metal hook at the end. Alan suspected that it was probably used for lifting engines and not men, as Wolf had led him to believe.

"Here's where we start, then. Get'cher clothes off." Alan looked at Wolf in disbelief. "I don't want to tell ya twice...strip'em." Alan took his clothes off, but without the initial wave of excitement. Wolf hooked his thumb at a tattered bucket seat, which looked like it had been pulled from some old Mustang. "Trust me, cowboy," he said. "This is just the first room." A greasy safety belt and shoulder harness went across the seat, then Wolf pulled polished heavy iron manacles from either side and from under the front. With expert ease, he had Alan locked into place.

So this is how a crash test dummy feels, Alan thought. But he also admitted that no-one had ever locked him up like this before. It had a definite fantasy air about it, being trapped with a kinky mechanic in a room full of grease and tools. Wolf stood before him, naked now except for his engineer boots, having lost the coveralls. He was holding a power box that dangled from a wire to the ceiling. "Think y'or safe and secure?"

"Yes Sir."

"Guess again." Wolf hit a green button on the power box and Alan felt the car seat begin to move. Alan realized it was on a track and motor, and was being pulled slowly toward the wall, but with his wrists and ankles locked down, there was no way to get out. The chair picked up speed and slid across the room, but before he could hit the wall, Alan saw a panel move aside as the seat whipped into another chamber.

The lights came up and Wolf's fantasy room was revealed. Laid out in front of Alan were all manner of metal cages and boxes, chains on pulleys, chains against the walls, anchor rings in the floor, an absolutely wicked looking torture rack, and in an area that wasn't so industrial clean, some large equipment that he couldn't identify. All of it was mirror bright and all of it looked like it could keep even a superman in place. Alan started getting nerv- ous as Wolf strode from machine to machine, pride-fully stoking the chrome restraints and the metal grid work. The big man turned to him and said with a big smile "Now do ya understand why my house is so simple? I spend all my time out here dreaming up devices and then figuring out how to build 'em. Then if I'm lucky, I find someone like y'all and I get to try 'em out. I've even got some new ones that no-one's seen yet." He strutted over behind Alan in the bucket seat and put his massive hands on Alan's shoulders. Alan felt those strong fingers dig into his flesh when Wolf asked, "Which one do ya want to play with first?"

Now Alan was getting scared. What he could identify was beyond anything he'd ever been turned on by, and what he couldn't figure out scared him even worse. He felt cold sweat start coming up on his chest when Wolf lowered his hands to Alan's nipples and started to pinch them roughly.

"C'mon cowboy. I ain't got all night and the Wolf's getting pretty hungry."

Alan made a quick decision. "Sir, I've never been on a rack before. Could we please try that?" He figured that if he didn't give Wolf an answer soon, he may find himself on one of those untried new machines Wolf was itching to test. Wolf undid the seat harness and unlocked the manacles, lifting Alan to his feet. Then Alan started to really freak when Wolf pushed him away from the rack he'd seen and over to a much more diabolical looking table.

"Since you've never ridden a rack before, let me start y'all out on the improved model." Wolf pushed Alan back-first into an X-shaped frame. Metal clamps automatically closed on Alan's wrists and ankles, and the hiss of air accompanied a cushion that filled the leftover space between the metal and Alan's flesh. Wolf pulled a wide leather belt across Alan's gut and fastened it shut, effectively pinning him to the middle of the table. "You look like one hot butterfly there, cowboy," Wolf said as he stepped away. He grasped a control box that was suspended from the ceiling, similar to the one that operated the car seat controls. "That other rack is one of the first things I ever built. I modeled it after one I saw in some movie, but it wouldn't do everything I wanted it to. So I sat down, drew this one out and built it to how I expected a rack to work. Now I can make each arm or leg move a little at a time..."

He pushed a button in the corner of the control box and Alan felt his right arm pullout an inch..."or have them all move the same distance at the same time." Alan felt all his limbs move at once as Wolf pressed the button in the center of the box. "And I can adjust yer arms and legs to an X-angle or straight up and down. Me, I like the X myself. It's more fun to watch ya squirm when all yer limbs are going in different directions." Another push to the control box's center button. There was a gear grinding sound and Alan felt his limbs go out to where there wasn't any slack. "What d'ya think?"

"Very good Sir!" Alan gasped. He was no longer scared of Wolf. He was getting terrified. Wolf wasn't just playing with S/M here. He was a fucking mad scientist!

"Excellent answer, cowboy! Let me show ya one other thing about this one." Wolf pulled a bar out and across the rack above Alan's waist. Three chains hung from it and Wolf began fastening them to Alan's body. A chrome ring was locked around Alan's cock and balls and then a pair of nipple clamps were secured. "What happens now is, since yer body's slowly being stretched away from the center of the table, every little bit you move pulls against these..." slapping the thin chains for emphasis..."And you're really getting it from seven directions instead of just four."

Wolf pushed the center button again. Alan felt his limbs pull out beyond their natural limit, but he also got a feel for what Wolf just described, a horrifying reverse pull against his nipples and groin as they crept away from the center of the device! He groaned as he realized that if Wolf really wanted him in agony, there was no way to stop him. And from the sound of things, Wolf wasn't just in this for a few moments of torment foreplay. This guy was a true sadist.

Another grinding sound and Alan felt his limbs pull just a fraction further, a fraction enough to make him yell. Wolf's face lit up. "Now that's what I like, a hot man who recognizes his pain! Now you just relax for a moment. You're gonna be surprised by how far out those arms and legs of yours can go. Same for your tits."

The frightening thing was, Alan realized, Wolf wasn't joking. He wondered what men who knew they were going to be drawn and quartered thought about before the executioner slapped the horses. Even worse, Alan could feel his joints settling down, even though the pain in his chest and crotch continued relentlessly.

Wolf pushed the button again and the grind signaled another fractional pull on Alan's limbs. The big man only laughed at Alan's screams and showed his own excitement by rubbing Alan's torture sensitive cock. "You think this is bad? Wait till you see what else I got in store for you. Get ready, cowboy. I'm gonna give you a ride like your buddies back in LA. only dream about. One more for round one."

The grinding noise was buried by Alan's garbled screams, animal howls of pain, his stretched limbs conflicting with the sex pain in his balls and tits. Although Alan was fully aware of the pain, he was also increasingly aware of his erection. Even through his terror, Wolf was making him hard. Suddenly, a slow hiss as the restraints retracted to their starting positions. Alan felt the warm relief in his joints as the muscles tried to re-gather themselves. Wolf's huge hands began gently massaging the shoulders and armpits, getting the heat circulating across the stretched out flesh. But the relief was only momentary; he grabbed the tit-clamps and popped them off Alan's tits so suddenly that Alan couldn't even suck in air to cry out.

As Alan tried to absorb the pain, Wolf was unfastening the wrist and ankle restraints, leaving the cock ring on his groin but disconnecting the lead. Alan's cock bounced back into place as the big man scooped him up off the table. "It's all right, Cowboy. Wolf ain't gonna hurt ya anymore." Wolf was rocking Alan back and forth, like he was trying to ease him to sleep. That big bush of a moustache brushed against Alan's ear as he repeatedly whispered. Over and over, "Wolf ain't gonna hurt ya anymore." He carried Alan over to a large chrome frame that was suspended alone in the center of the room. A lace work of leather crossed inside the metal frame, like a hammock.

Alan felt himself almost delicately laid into this soft bed of leather, and was too weak to resist when Wolf fastened additional strips of leather around his extremities, holding him face down, but comfortably, in place. Wolf's big arms swung the cables that held the frame, letting it sway gently with Alan restrained inside. "From now on, Cowboy tortures himself. How much do you like electricity?"

Alan could only moan in response. Wolf's hand pulled the cock ring between a space in the leather webbing, bringing Alan's dick below the frame. Since his head was below the chrome case that made up the surrounding rectangle of his netting, he could only see Wolf's actions from below the leather. He watched as a rolling metal cart was pushed below him, and as Wolf turned a hand crank till the top of the table barely touched Alan's erection. There was a shiny disc atop the cart's tray, with wires leading below. Although Alan couldn't see where the wires led, he had a pretty good idea. Wolf took another wire from under the tray and fastened it to the chrome cock ring.

"I don't have to hurt you anymore, cowboy. You want your pain so bad that you're going to have a hard-on until you stop wanting it." He gave the frame another push and Alan could feel the head of his dick brush the metal disk each time he passed back over it. "So if you want the torture to stop, you can do it one of two ways. Swing yourself away from that chrome tray..." Alan felt his cock head brush the disk again..."Or go soft enough so you don't make the connection." Wolf's hands grabbed the frame and he steadied it till Alan's cock rested atop the tray once more.

Wolf settled himself into a black leather car seat with a chrome frame; almost the match for the frame and webbing Alan was captivated by. Alan could only see Wolf from the hips down, and for the first time, saw his tormentor's erect cock. It was a beer can monster, surrounded by a thick thatch of hair as black as the man's moustache. It swelled out to a piston-like six inches of circumference, and the sight of it made Alan as excited and as terrified as ever.

Above Alan's sight range, Wolf had his grip on another of his suspended control boxes, and he pushed the green button on it, then a start-up sound of a low grade hum from the table tray resting below Alan's frame. "That's right, cowboy. On this ride, you have to make it stop all by yerself. Let me tell ya something else." Wolf turned a dial on his control box to increase the power flowing between the cock ring and the chrome disk. "It makes one hell of a difference when you get some pre-cum in that cock of yours."

Alan suddenly felt the first stabbing pulse of electricity zap him from the base of his cock and balls to the tip of his circuit completing cock head. It was almost like a sinister upgrade of Edgar Alan Poe, except Alan had become trapped on the pendulum instead of underneath it. He jerked and twisted until he had the frame moving in a steady rhythm back and forth above the table, but there was no escaping the return swing, and each touch brought another jolt and another shout of agony.

"Something else I didn't tell you," Alan heard Wolf say. "The longer you stay off the tray top, the more the shock increases. No connection, more power. Took me weeks to figure out the circuitry."

"You bastard! Let me up, you son of a bitch!"

"Aww cowboy, that ain't no way to talk to the man who's saving you an impound fee. I'm sure that even though it's dark, my Daddy's already towed your car off to the junkyard before the cops even got a look at your license plates."

The implication sank in. Alan was trapped here, his abandoned car already hidden away so no evidence of being here existed. He could see Wolf's incredible erection from his torture table as wave after wave of short sharp shocks hammered at his cock, and he remembered again what Wolf had told him just before turning on the power...

"...Or go soft enough so you don't make the connection."

That's when Alan realized that, as horrible as this madman's imagination was, or as diabolical as the devices Wolf dreamed up and built, he still hadn't lost his erection. The torture was no longer limited to his dick, either. Sweat bursting from his body was also conducting shocks everywhere there was moisture. Wolf wasn't lying about the power increase, Alan's futile swinging of the frame away from the plate was driving the intensity of shocks incrementally higher, and the exertion was making him sweat harder. As Wolf sat across from him, leisurely stroking himself, Alan was entertaining him without his having to get up from his chair! And no matter how much he fought it, the shocks were getting more and more painful as his cock got hotter and hotter, the sweat and pre-cum adding to the intensity of the hurt!

Time, agony and pleasure were all a blur to Alan now, even though his screams were drowning out any other possible sound. It must have given Wolf all the satisfaction he could handle in one setting, because suddenly, Alan felt his cock head drag across the sweaty tray top and not receive a stab of electricity in response. He stopped fighting to make the frame swing and began to catch his breath, when he heard Wolf's voice from above him.

"You sure are one hot pain pig there, cowboy. I think maybe it's time we called it a night. I gotta get you to El Paso tomorrow, remember?"

"You mean you really aren't out to kill me?"

"Shit, no. I told you before we started, I love control, chrome and I like things to get scary. C'mon cowboy, I didn't have you scared, did I?"

Alan felt himself feeling sort of stupid, "Well, yes Sir."

The big man smiled at this. "Get over here, cowboy." He wrapped those ham hock sized arms around Alan and gave him a bear of a hug. Alan noticed that Wolf still hadn't lost his hard-on, but that was okay by him. "Then you ready to go back in the house?"

"Yes Sir."

Wolf pulled that hug even tighter and picked Alan off the ground, but he jammed him against a thick square of wood, duct tape suddenly appearing and binding him to its length. A musty tasting rag was shoved into his mouth and tape trapped it inside. "Still scared, cowboy?"

Alan felt the log get lifted onto a long narrow table and turned on its side. Wolf started to position it lengthwise. "Let me tell ya about my favorite old time movie scene. There was always this abandoned logging mill where the hero would get tied up by the bad guy, and he had to find a way to escape the table saw before the bad guy sliced him in half." Wolf lifted a cover from the end of the table, revealing a massive, evil looking circular blade, polished up shiny, with teeth that jutted out at queer sideways angles. "The out door is on the other side of the table, cowboy. Ready for one last ride?"

Alan tried screaming and busting loose from the tape, but he had absolutely no slack at all to work from. With another one of his loud laughs, the big man said "Duct tape gets tighter the more you fight it. I bought three of these blades from a sawmill that was shutdown about ten years ago, polished them up and I've been using them ever since." Wolf took yet another control box, this one with three sets of buttons on it and pushed the first set. With a deafening roar, a ventilation fan turned on, sucking air and dust towards the ceiling. The second green button started the blade turning, the vicious teeth spinning in a blur of motion. The third jerked Alan's log, pushing him feet first, on his side, nearer to the cutting edge of the saw.

Even as he screamed and fought, he looked over and saw Wolf furiously jacking himself, and as the first sounds of metal tearing wood began, Alan realized that the vibrations were even tingling his own cock. Through his fear, he watched that massive mountain of a man pulling himself wildly as the belt pushed the wood block deeper into the dangerous bite of the blade, Alan feeling the ice cold terror as the blade ripped the duct tape like tissue and the sensations moved through his legs and knees, behind his body and along his back, not to mention the earth shattering shake as the blade moved through the wood against his ass.

As it did, he heard Wolf's mammoth howl as he shot

streams of jiz while the blade finished its evil trek though the board Alan was still taped to, even as it was halved. Alan rolled to one side, the board still fastened on top of him and moving along the belt, though a set of flaps and into another room. He could hear as the fan, saw, and belt were shut down and then as Wolf walked into the room, his cock still dribbling through the foreskin.

"The door to the house is on this side of the wall, cowboy." Wolf yanked the gag out of Alan's mouth and cut the remaining duct tape from his body. Alan fell limp from the board, and Wolf lifted him to his feet. "You can spend the night in two places. Either in my bed in the house or out here in the guest bed...with me of course." Wolf flashed those animal eyes again. "If Y'all come in the house, the two of us go to El Paso. Stay out here, and I'll see ya when I get home. I'll let you out of a chrome bar cell and I'll forge you the hottest collar a man ever locked on ya. You said it yerself, maybe the high and mighty don't want ya living in Texas. What's it gonna be, cowboy?"

Alan hesitated. He saw Wolfs eyes suddenly fill with doubt. It was a sight so sad that even he couldn't turn the big man away. He thought about a big old desert rat, dreaming up hot toys and devices, building them in the heat of passion, lust, and desert night. Realizing the man's loneliness when he saw them sitting complete yet empty, like an only child with the best toy box who couldn't stop longing for someone to play with. Alan made his decision.

"Have a good drive, Sir," was all he needed to say.

HE THINKS OF ME AS "HIM"

My former Master probably thinks of me from time to time. Everyone has their first teacher, and he was mine. After all, he initiated me into rubber and SM, when I was still no more than some ignorant greenhorn with an interest of rough sex. I saw him interacting with men at the Jailbreak Bar I had just started going to, back when all I had was a pair of rubber boots and latex leggings. I knew what I was looking for, but was fearful about approaching someone towards the effect of doing anything about it. He stood against the brick railing of the bar, all confidence and braggadocio, chatting with casual animation. While I had already befriended a couple of the other Leathermen in the bar, this man was someone new. My train of thought was if these people were already at ease with Him (I was already thinking of Him in uppercase letters), then He must be an experienced player in the city. There I stood, just allowing the conversations to flow around each other, when He made a joke about someone who ran scared when He suggested that he would take the inquisitor home to tie up and beat on for sex. The other men laughed about it, but I felt my own dick go rock hard at the thought. At the first opportunity I could, after the other men had wandered off for a moment, I introduced myself to Him and brazenly asked "Sir, would you take me home and beat on me?"

He looked at me with one eyebrow arched. Then He replied, flipping me a business card, "Not tonight, pup. I'm tired. If you're still serious, call me tomorrow afternoon and we'll talk about it. By the way, nice boots, boy."

I was astounded. Here was the most confident looking Top I'd ever seen, the first I'd ever even approached about my fantasies and He complimented me on my rubber boots. Maybe I hesitated just, a little too long, because He turned and strutted out the door before I could utter a proper "Thank you, Sir" in reply. But I could feel my fingers already sweating around the tiny card in my hand. I most certainly would call Him the next day. I returned to my meager apartment and although it took many tosses and turns to get there, I eventually fell into a restless sleep.

When I woke up, there was no lingering drowsiness. My cock was already stiffened by excitement, and I was afraid to jerk off if it meant displeasing this man I'd only exchanged those couple of sentences with at the Jailbreak. I turned to see what time it was, the red l.e.d.'s flashed 6:30. My eagerness was so far off the scale that I'd only slept a few hours! My listlessness continued, as much as I wanted to stay in bed for a while longer, there was no way I was going to fall back to sleep. There was a full five hours to kill before I could even consider phoning Him. The business card was placed directly next to the phone at bedside. I read it and reread it like it was scripture. Or a mantra to be repeated. I also remembered His order that I wait until afternoon to call. I wanted it, I needed it, and if timing was that important to Him, I could wait till later, barely.

If nothing else, I could at least waste a few moments on how I would look when He asked me to come over. He had already complimented the boots, so they were a given. Should I try to replicate the look I had last night or try something else? I had no idea what this man was all about, just that His motorcycle reverberated out of the parking lot as I stood inside the bar dumbfounded. But since He had already given me some kind of acceptance by acknowledging me in the bar, I decided that at the very least, I'd begin with the boots and then the leggings. What of a shirt? Should it be black clothes? I had a blue dress military shirt, but it certainly didn't go with the rubber pants. Something told me that while He may not give a whit about fashion, He would definitely be aware of form and function. I chose a solid black, logo-less t-shirt, no holes or tears, with sleeves. So much for dressing.

7:15. I Had to admit, I looked hot. After all, I thought, I was young, pretty good looking, well toned, new in the city...date bait material for sure! I bet myself that I could score with any Top in town. But that wasn't what I wanted. There was just something about Him, and I had to know. So I watched the digits click by on the clock. Till 8:00, 9:00 and eventually 11:00 blinked by. Then finally, 12:00, but was it still too early to call? He did say "afternoon," and to me that usually meant later in the day. But I couldn't help myself. I was sweating enough as it was from the waiting. 12:04, I picked up the phone, looked at the card, and went for broke. One ring, Two, Three, Click "Hello." Not a question, but a statement, all business, all confidence.

"Umm, hello Sir, I'm Daniel, the boy you met at Jailbreak last night?"

A slight laugh on the other line. "Ah yes, the pup with the rubber boots. You remembered to call, very good. Shows you have some discipline so far."

"You did ask me to, Sir. Would you still like me to come to you this afternoon?" He answered in the affirmative, and I could feel my stomach erupt in butterflies. He gave me the directions to His house and told me be there inside the hour...and I was in the car sixty seconds after I hung up the phone, maybe even quicker.

When I got there, the first thing He did was slip my rubber pants down below my crotch. "Just wanted to satisfy my curiosity, pup. Go get in the shower and take that shirt off. Nothing else, just the shirt." His voice was so commanding that questioning His order wasn't even an option. I went to the stand-up shower in His bathroom and He soon stood before me, in a harness and rubber shorts that had a snap-away codpiece. He pushed me to the back of the stall and undid His flap, revealing a beautiful, multi-pierced dick, which He aimed directly at the tops of my rubber boots. I forced myself not to flinch, and thanked myself for not wearing socks. "Very good, pup. You've got the makings of a first class slut in you." He pulled me away from the shower stall and into His bedroom, where a large four poster bed waited. Backed against the closest pillar, at the foot of the bed. A set of handcuffs were placed on my wrists behind the post, clicked into some kind of ring there, then two leather straps appeared to crisscross my chest. I was secured by a man who I was a total stranger to, but felt complete trust in...and realized that I was about to realize my long held fantasy. This was the man who was finally going to grant me my first journey into the realm of SM. "I like your taste in pants, pup. I don't wear my rubber out much, leather goes better on my bike. But I like the way it makes you sweat. And with me, you'd better be ready to sweat."

His tones were so deep and so musical that although I recognized it as an order, He may as well been singing to me. He even hummed slightly to himself as He began rummaging through a few toys in the cabinet next to the bed. Tit clamps came out, as did a narrow dildo and bottle of lube, and several long rolls of rubber. He held the dildo up to my face and asked if I'd ever had much experience with ass-play. "No Sir." He smiled. "Then prepare to get serious, pup. From here on in, you say nothing. Everything I ask you, you'll be able to answer by nodding. You speak, story's over. Got that, pup?" I gave an Affirmative nod. "Fast learner, pup, I like that." He took the bottle of lube and pumped some on to the rubber phallus, still only inches from my face. As He rubbed the slick liquid along the dildo, He told me just how tightly His toy was going to fit next to my rubber pants and that I should be thinking about how He was going to feel in there when He thought I was ready for it. With little fanfare, He slid my pants below my ass and began slowly screwing the dildo into its new home. I felt the rubber begin a gentle twisting as it slid up my chute, I was paralyzed against the bedpost, Him humming and enjoying himself. The dildo in up to its foundation, He slid a thong through the ball shaped base which fastened to a rubber cock-ring that He then secured around front. He lifted the pants back into place with a smile and a flourish. "Every time you move, you'll get a little reminder of who put you where you are now. Got it, pup?" I nodded; I could feel the twinge in my butt as my dick got harder.

He took the tit-clamps and opened them as wide as they could go, and began pinching my nipples with His fingers. Harder and harder, until I began to mince and gasp with the pain. "Good pup," He muttered into my ear, "good pup." His words twisted in my mind, He was hurting me and congratulating me for it at the same time...was this what it was about? The tit clamps were fastened in place, they were less pinching then His fingers were. I tried to catch my breath, He looked me in the face and warned me "I'm going to make sure these stay in place, pup. Ready?" I nodded and He clicked a ratchet that squeezed the clamps down tighter. I jumped against the bedpost, my cock and balls pulled against the cock-ring and the dildo jerked in response. My rubber boots were sloshing. It was all I could do not to cry out. "Now, now pup, this is why you came, right?" I nodded yes and He cradled my head and stroked my hair. "Good pup." My eyes were watering while He continued reassuring me. My cock stayed hard through it all. "Good pup."

He picked up the rubber straps and began turning them against the bed post. My shoulders were pulled even more securely to the pillar, my handcuffed wrists anchored all the more firmly. He left an opening where the tit-clamps were before tucking the end of the strip behind my back. Then He surprised me once again by notching the tit-clamps one degree tighter...whereupon I did shout. "You okay, pup?" This time I had to reply... "Please Sir; I've never done this before." Now it was His turn to look surprised. "Never, pup?" I nodded no. I was shaking, the dildo was teasing my prostate gland to its edge, the cock-ring was squeezing my ball sac to its limits, and the tit-clamps were hot wired down to my dick. He smiled. "Pup, you're taking to it real well. When you're done here today, you're coming back to me next weekend. Got that, pup?" I emphatically nodded yes. The pain/pleasure was driving me to shakes that my bound body could do nothing about, and He pulled out His pierced beauty to show me the effect it was having on Him. "Pup, I let you cum and you'll feed on this. Understood?" I nodded yes again; actually, I don't think I ever stopped nodding. I wanted His cock that much. He didn't even take my dick out from the cock-ring or the shorts; He just kept massaging the front of my rubber pants with one hand and gliding His thumb over my left nipple with His other. "C'mon pup. Show your new Master why you're here." Those words were like the secret code I needed to hear, and my rubber leggings flooded with jerk after jerk of cum, leaving Him smiling and me gasping for breath. "Good pup," He said over and over, "Good pup." He unwound the rubber strapping, removed the harness, released the handcuffs and took off the tit-clamps. (I screamed when He did that, He just rubbed my too sensitive nipples and said "Don't worry pup. You'll get used to it.") but

Freed at last and on my knees, He gave me one more set of instructions. "Please your new Master. Got that, pup?" I sure did, and He got the Master's lick of a lifetime. Before I left, He had a slave's contract in my pocket. "If you're still serious, pup, have that committed to memory, signed and in my hands by 7pm Friday. Got it, pup?" Big nod of yes!

Next week He had what He wanted, a signed contract from my hands as I knelt before Him, a rubber slave at His beckon call every weekend. On more than a few week nights, too. He was a most patient Rubber Master, teaching me how to make friends with His pain, showing me how He liked to be treated, teaching me His concepts of rubber slave etiquette. This continued for seven more months... until the company I worked for announced my pro-motion. It seems that they noticed how much better a worker I had become in the last half year. The job was out of state, but the pay raise was incredible! I couldn't wait to break the news to Master. I knew He would be proud of His pup and his success. I guess I was just a bit too young or foolish. Because for the first time, as I stood next to His bed, preparing to turn out the light and before He would padlock my rubber collar to a chain attached to the bedpost, I saw my Master cry. I asked Him the question He instructed me to give every night before lights out. "Is there any-thing else you wish for, Sir?"

"Yes pup. A bottom that would stay here for me."

My heart was breaking as He pulled me into His arms and began sticking me with His vampire gloves, the toys I knew He loved the most.

Still, I was feeling just a little selfish, thinking (being young and cocky) that there were plenty of men just like Him in whatever city I would land. But I was so wrong. It's been four years now since we first met, and I haven't met anyone with the kind of per-sonal code of ethics He embodied. We kept up with each other for a year or so, I even went back to visit Him once or twice, but it was never the same. My job keeps me busy, His next slave moved in with Him and He picked up another boy shortly there-after. I always hoped He would be happy with an extended family,

He Thinks of Me as "Him"

as the letters and calls drew farther and longer apart...and eventually disappeared altogether, I realized something about my particular bond that saddens me everyday since.

My former Rubber Master probably thinks of me from time to time, I'm sure. But He no longer thinks of me as "pup."

He thinks of me as "Him."

NINE TENTHS OF THE LAW

MY BEST FANTASIES INCLUDE FRAMING PEOPLE FOR MY OWN PLEASURE.

I just know what I enjoy, much if not most of it would be considered non-sexual. A good mind fuck or screwing somebody's daily life for my own enjoyment never fails to get me hard. (Tears are so much more satisfying than screams.) It is possible to fuck with people using existing system rigmarole or bureaucratic bullshit. I work extensively with the criminal justice system so I know exactly what a cop like me can pull to fuck with people. I like placing bogus warrants for people in a bureaucratic machine and then setting them up to be arrested. No origination, no way to trace it, and they're fucked for at least 72 hours. Simple stuff like that. Not particularly sexy, but a LOT of fun.

I'm saying this cause I just saw the next person I want to feel my own special brand of humiliation. He was cruising the bar and being just a little too arrogant. All attitude, blond hair begging to get sheared off, with a tight gym body. Just fucking begging to be taken down a peg or two. He wouldn't give anyone in the bar the time of day. He was too busy trying to prove he could take or leave the whole joint behind even if everyone in the place wanted him. I wanted him too, but he just breezed right on by me and didn't give me more than a passing glance. His first mistake. His second was parking real close to the bar. Getting his license plate as he pulled away from the curb was a cinch. He may have acted like some untouchable Leather Adonis, but I knew how to find him. In twenty four hours, I would have his name on a document and he was going to be getting a personal in uniform visit from me and my "unmarked" car. You don't punk an entire bar while I'm in it and walk away. If this boy didn't know how already, I wanted to make him learn terror, and I had just the plan to help him live the word.

Run the plates: an address for "Peter B. Mills." That was easy enough; Spotless record, even better! Good part of town; I was liking Mr. Mills more and more. Probably some punk that thought his money spared him from any of the world's shit. He didn't know that by 1700 hour I'd be cuffing him inside his house and accusing him of being a cop killer. Not just any cop, my partner! Just the kind of situation that might transform Officer Friendly into a revenge seeking maniac. Mr. Mills probably still lives in a fantasy world where police officers helped small children cross the street and would be interested if the neighbors' dog crapped on his yard. My new goal is to take Mr. Mills to the other side of the tracks and show him what a man with 25 years on the force turns into when he arrests the slimy fuck who killed his best bud. Thinking about it gets me real hard. I decide to do a drive by.

Idyllic as hell. Nice yards, pretty flowers. I could get into stomping my boots in Mr. Mills grass just to piss him off. His house was all too perfect; white siding, tile roof, bay windows, single story, basement, driveway with garage, and a Basement stairwell leading up to the driveway. Good place to start the evening. I begin thinking about what Mr. Perfect was going to do once I start trashing his basement looking for "the drugs." I bet the guy never touched the shit, so just being accused would make him piss himself.

I wonder what Mr. Mills will think about a ride in the trunk of my car. It's pretty greasy back there. Betcha he'll have on his office shirt when I show up. Fucking with this arrogant S.O.B. is gonna be fun.

Its 1700 hour and I'm backing into Mr. Mills' driveway, taking care to aim my trunk at that basement stairwell. I take out my gun, badge and warrant (issued that day) and approach the door. Ring the doorbell and knock real hard...it should rattle him. It does, he doesn't even ask who's there, he just throws the door open. Ahh, the power of the uniform! I flash my badge, blurt my name and tell him I have a warrant for his arrest . He goes whiter than snow. Starts babbling about some kind of mistake as I barge through the door. Before he can say anything else, I slam the door and shove him against the wall.

"I know you did it asshole," I snarl at him. "You killed my partner when he caught you with the crystal. If you think your scum bag lawyer can get you off this one, you're full of shit." Sweat starts to bead on Mr. Mills already. His perfect hair is slipping. His attitude from the bar has already vanished like a fucking cloud of smoke. I turn him around and cuff him real tough. "Oh yeah. Something else." I push my gun into the little weasel's spinal cord. "You have the right to remain silent..." jamming him face first into the wall harder as I continue his Miranda, and ramming my knee between his legs as I wrap it up with"...something my partner doesn't have anymore."

Mills gasps, "I didn't do anything! I didn't do anything!" I spin him back around to face me, throwing his cuffed hands into the wall. He yells real loud. I like it!

"Where's the speed, shit head." Mills looks at me with his eyes wide open. I pull him away from the wall and jam him back into it. "I said, where's the speed?" He doesn't answer, so I grab him by his collar and drag him around his house, room by room and violently knock shit off tables. I know there won't be any dope here, but he doesn't know that I know. All he knows is throb in his balls and pissed off cop in his face. I get to a place I want him; throw him down on his bed, start in on the drawers and then his closet till I find what I'm really looking for. Better yet, his handcuffs are still hanging off the side clip. Yanking the hanger out of the closet, I wave black leather chaps in his direction.

"So what's this, asshole? You wear these to the bars? They make your buns tight? Huh? You dangerous? You like it rough? You're gonna think anything you've done till now was recess on the fucking playground." I pull him off the bed and get my mirror shades and moustache close as his nose will let me. He stinks of fear-sweat. "Cause I'm not going to let you within screaming distance of a slime bucket lawyer until you tell me how you killed my partner, why you killed him and what you did with the crystal. And I'll kill you before I let some chunk of shit in a tie get you out of jail." I knock my forehead against his and let his sweat hit against my skin. He's hot when he's terrified, I think to myself.

"Let's make this real easy. We'll start with where in the house do you have the drugs? You have some real fancy shit in here. It would really suck if I started smashing it."

Mills' face is dripping clammy sweat. I grab his cheeks with one leather gloved hand and squeeze his mouth open. He's been clamoring that he doesn't know what I'm talking about and let him go and it'll just take one phone call, nothing too original. "By the time I'm through with you, this hole won't be able to stay shut." I grab him by the collar again and drag him down his basement stairs. Just as I thought, this anal retentive jerk has an immaculate tool bench and it's completely cleaned off. I undo one of the cuffs then relock it to a corner of the table, and start throwing shit around, all the while yelling at Mills "Where's the drugs?" over and over, louder and louder. I'm getting real worked up over all this and it's having both the desired effects. He's getting even more scared and my dick ain't gone soft. I stop smashing long enough to walk over to Mills and stare. There's a claw hammer on the bench where I dumped a box. I pick it up and start hitting my palm with it. I let my voice go deep and slow as I repeat once more. "Where are the drugs?"

"Please Sir, I don't have any drugs. Don't hit me, please don't hit me."

"Oh no," I growl. "I wouldn't hit you with the hammer. I'm going to pull your pants down and shove the handle up your ASS!" At which point I scream as loud as I fucking can and start swinging the hammer into the work bench, slamming it for all I'm worth and roaring like an insane animal. Mills' muscle body is pulling the tool bench hard enough to lift it, matching me scream for hammer blow, even without me laying a finger on him. I stop bashing the bench and look at him, breathing hard. He's shaking like a leaf. Inside I'm laughing like crazy. He's mine!

I see a coil of rope in with the junk I've dumped on the floor. I pick it up and cut a couple of lengths from it. Pushing Mills against the table, I tie his ankles together, then I unlock the handcuffs and tie his hands in front of him. "We're gonna take a ride. Not gonna take you to the station. I got a special place downtown

where you and me are gonna get to know each other real well.
You and me are gonna get closer than any friend you ever had..."
I take the hammer and throw it as hard as I can into the wall. I
almost shoot a load as I pick Mills up over my shoulder, cart him
up the steps outside the basement and literally dump him into the
trunk of my car. Before I shut the hatch, I tell him "Think of it this
way. I've already let you live longer than you gave my partner. I
must be getting soft." Mills gets one last look at my mirror shades
as I throw the hood down with a satisfying slam and get in the driver's seat.

I take the long way round, cruise the expressway, just to
make sure Mills is disoriented by the time I get him downtown.
I've kept a loft space for the last few years, complete with a loading bay door and 20 foot high ceilings. Room enough for a couple
of cells, a great bondage table and a hot room just for dickheads
like Mills. A long wooden table, a couple of desk chairs with solid
wooden arms, and one of them on casters, so it'll roll around. One
wall covered with a huge mirror to make most of my prisoners
think it might be a two way, if I need to give some twit the impres-
sion that he's being observed. But that isn't what I have in mind
for Mr. Mills.

I pull the car alongside the loading bay door and watch it
lift. Then I go back and bang on the trunk lid a couple of times.
"Hope you been thinking of something to say, asshole," I yell at the
metal. "I ain't in the mood for bullshit." There isn't a sound from
behind the metal, so I make a big deal out of putting the key into
the lock and popping the trunk. Mills has pushed himself back as
far as he could, but so fucking what? I get my uniformed arm in
there and pull him out like a sack of dog food. I throw him over
the edge of the loading dock and hit the door button. It comes
down behind me as I jump in the loft. Mills is lying on the floor in
front of me, still tightly rope bound. He's got a shiner from the ride
here. Yeah...hot. I poke at him with my polished hip boot. He
flinches, even though all I did was bump him with my toe. Mills
can only look up at me from below, up at an outfit that all his life
has meant nothing but power and protection from the bad guys.
"What's the matter, asshole? Worried I might give you a good
kick? Not yet...you still might need that rib cage for later, see?"

I pull him up, he's looking real bad. His hair is allover the place, the office shirt is caked in sweat and trunk grease, and his eyes aren't so full of 'cocky' anymore. I push him into the wooden chair with the casters and spin him in circles. " Take a good look around shit head. See all that stuff? You wanna find out how it's all used? You think those handcuffs on your chaps made you bad? Shouldn't wear 'em if you don't know how to use 'em, because now I'm your worst nightmare, I'm the cop who won't stop when you cry uncle. I'm the man who doesn't care if uniforms, handcuffs and chains give you a hard-on. I'm the cop whose part-ner you shot and I don't give a rat's ass if I take you out of here in irons or a body bag. So tell me what I wanted to know back at your rich druggy house and maybe I won't crush you." I take the chair and aim it at the mirror. "That ain't a two way like in the movies. Detectives aren't behind it watching us. Maybe I have a camera back there taking a video of you, so I can play it over when I think about my partner. You'll never know that, will you?"

Pulling his hair back, Mills is forced to stare into it. "Look at yourself. All that pretty stuff your money bought you doesn't look so hot now. You don't look like you're hotter than anyone else in town. I'm your new special friend, and I want you to think about what someone on his way to the gas chamber looks like." My chest and elbow forces his head into an unmovable position as I grab a battery powered razor and start shearing him. Those locks start falling to the floor and his head starts getting shiny. It only takes a few minutes, twisting and squirming, tied tight and muscle held in my chair, to turn Mills into a cue ball. I spin him around to face the mirror so he can see his new look. "They shave you so you can't slip the head harness. Now start telling what I need to hear so you at least have a chance at the Governor letting you off the hook. Because I don't plan on letting you out of this room until I get what I need and I abso-fucking-lutely do not care how long it takes." I roll the chair hard and fast into the wall. He comes away with a bloody lip. I pre-cum more.

Mills is whimpering like a whipped pup. "I didn't do it man. I didn't do anything."

I fake a big dramatic sigh. "Guess I'll have to show you a

few of my favorite tools, then. " I push the chair into the table and it knocks the formerly blond punk to the floor. "Get the fuck up!" And I yank him onto the table. I spread his shoes across one end and spread eagle his feet, then untie his wrists and jerk him into a full spread eagle. It's big, old, and solid weighty oak, heard all manner of screams, but I got the feeling this night's going to be special. Once I get my punk to the point where he can't do much moving, I start showing off the tools. One of them is a big assed western Bowie knife and I push it under his shirt, ripping towards his throat. "Don't want to go too fast here, bud. I got other things I wanna put around that pretty boy neck of yours." I grab the shirt and rip it off his chest, and I gotta admit, this punk has a fine body on him. The money he spent on a gym membership was obviously being put to good use. I make a mental note of some ideas for that stomach and move on. "See this?" I ask, waving a leather hood over his head. "I bet a tough leather punk like you wears 'em all the time. Since you don't want to talk to me, your best new friend in the whole world, you're gonna wear this for awhile. No sight, no sound, no speaking. For the next 120 minutes, nothing but whatever I make you feel. Got that asshole?

"Just remember one thing. When I take the plugs out of your ears, be very fucking afraid. When I allow you to hear, every step you hear me make, every creak of my gun leather, anything will bring you some sort of pain. You can't tell when, where or how much, but if you hear me move, you will experience something uncomfortable. Got it asshole?" I open a humidor I keep for special events and pull out a Honduran. I exaggerate the hell out of lighting it and blowing smoke all over that sweaty face of his. "You think about how hot the end of this cigar gets when I suck on it." With my mouth clamping down on my smoke, I stuff his ears with waxy cotton balls and then zip the hood over his head. I jam a plug gag into his mouth and start pumping it...till I know it's filling his mouth and pushing his tongue down hard. I take the nose tube and wave the butterfly valve in front of his eyes, and for the hell of it, give it about a ten second pinch. My dick has stayed hard since I had him in the bedroom, but the look in Mills' eyes when he understood that my thumb and forefinger are his air supply makes me dribble. Then, with one more mouthful of smoke in his face, I wrap a strap of cloth over his eyes and knot it tight on the side of his head. I know he'll be able to feel his pulse under it, and that's just what I want. The last thing he's seeing is a uniformed stud with a cigar in his mouth, the last thing he's hearing is the near insane ravings of a madman, and the only thing he knows is that he ain't supposed to be here. He can't see, hear, move or even cry out, and Officer Friendly just turned into a homicidal Mr. Hyde with leather gloves on his air tube.

For a change I take advantage of this moment, he really is hot looking. I undo my zipper and stroke my dick, thinking about exactly where I want to start interrogating Mr. Mills. The muscles on his chest stretch and fall with each breath across the bondage table, and the thought of torturing him turns me on far more than the usual hostage I bring to my workshop. I promised Mills plenty of torment before I unblocked his ears, and even for assholes with pretty boy chips on their shoulders, this officer's word is still gold.

Still, I've already given him a few things to stew with. I give him the time to let the images and words sink in, enjoying my cigar and stroking my dick. Telling him about the gas chamber, planting the image of a red hot cigar coal, seeing his carefully cooked up image being knocked down by aiming his greasy expensive shirt and shaved head in the mirror while a perfectly presented hot uniformed cop forces him down the pretty boy ladder. For him, nothing else to interfere with his mind except the thoughts of the night so far. For me, a former attitude queen getting closer to rock bottom. My dick is starting to talk back to me...me knowing full well that if I'm going to take him all the way down and ten feet lower, I'll have to do at least one other thing. Mills may just need it. At least that's what my dick is telling me. He can stew in his juices, I could relax with mine. I would've given anything to read his mind under that shaved head and hood.

I rise up out of my chair and walk around my hostage. I wonder if he thinks this is what happens to all cop killers. He looks so good that I flick cigar ash on his chest. His first sensation since the hood went on. Mills jumps big from the sudden hot sting. It's time to start the slow build to screamland. I go to my wall rack and select a riding crop. This one has a soft leather tip. For beginners, I let the tip brush against each of his nipples and slide it between his tits. I rap his abs a couple of times, just to remind him about who is out there. Standing an arm's length away from his chest, the tapping begins. Not hard, just constant. I build the rhythm a little harder after about five minutes. No pain yet, just to let the touch sink in. This part of interrogation is sensation. I stop with the crop and move to the lower end of the table. I undo his shoelaces and strip his feet of patent leather and silk socks. Pulling up the chair and taking a few puffs on my cigar, I start with the tapping again, this time against the left foot. Not intensely, just constantly. His hood rolls from side to side, he knows my presence. Right foot, Tap tap tap tap...his toes arch and his arches bend. No pain, just feeling. I control the feelings. There is nothing else in his mind except the terror I've planted and he knows it. Left foot, harder this time, Tap tap tap tap   Once more to the right foot...tap tap tap tap...and I begin to play the pant legs. The crop works his shins harder, enough to sting under the cloth. Sound of tap becomes a sharper slap... slap... slap. Left shin, then right shin, a little further up the leg each time. He obviously knows my eventual destination now. I move from the tip of the crop to the actual shaft and start hitting the shins with more force. I can hear the cracks, even if he can't and it makes me chuckle.

Time for a different approach; The crop goes back on the wall for a leather paddle and the space between his thighs. I like knowing that Mills' pants are between his brain and my blows, one more thing to make him worry about. The idea of taking his balls out and bruising them is enticing. Maybe once I unstop his ears. For the first time, I lay a good hit on him, one across his chest. He arches. Hot! Hot enough for me to do it again! He twists. I love it! Third hit. I think I hear a noise from behind the gag. Good enough, I decide to add something new. I set an ashtray on the table next to Mills' head and rest my cigar in it. Then I set his nose tube next to the tip. I watch as curls of smoke work their way into the opening, grinning to myself knowing that they're on the way to Mills' lungs...with no way for him to breathe them away. This is the state I leave him in for a couple more minutes. I check my watch...two hours has passed pretty damn fast. I take my cigar away from the breath tube and listen as the rush of air slows to a normal rhythm again. Then I press my thumb over the open hole and look at my watch for the last 30 seconds of Mills' promised 120 minutes. I watch as his hands flail against the ropes and his feet jerk wildly. The second hand sweeps past the six on its way back to the twelve. Mills' hooded head is flying from side to side and my cock is ready to explode. Five, four, three, two, one...thumb away. Those chest muscles work hard to play catch up. It's time to take the ear plugs out and bring him up to a new level. I unzip the hood and pull the cotton balls away, the wax has made them into perfect positives of his ears. Zipping the hood back closed, I move into closer proximity and whisper one word into Mills' ear.

"Boo."

He jerks so hard that I think he may have raised the table. In spite of myself, I laugh out loud. I get in close again and whisper some more in his ear. "My partner and I served on the force for 25 years together. I don't even think you're that old. Remember what I told you before I stopped your ears? If you don't, let me remind you. After I stop talking, sound equals pain. Every step of my uniform's boots, every creak of belt leather, anything. You can't tell when, where or how much, but if you hear me move, you will hurt. I'm setting my watch for another 15 minutes, and after that your blindfold comes off. Fifteen more minutes, the gag and the hood. By then, you had better be ready to sing Starting from now."

Mill's lays perfectly still. I don't move, nothing for the first minute. I quietly pick up my cigar, which is about two thirds finished. I puff on it a few times and move my hand over his chest. My boot comes up from the floor. It stomps back down and just as it hits the concrete, I flick the ash. A thoroughly satisfying spasm from Mills as the singe goes through him. I take a pair of alligator clips and get them open near each nipple. I kick the table once and let the right one chomp tit. Kick the table again and the left clip bites raw skin. A tiny trickle of blood starts flowing from each side of his chest. I pick up the metal ashtray in my left hand and my crop in my right. The tray falls to the floor with a clang and the crop nails the shoulder. I kick the ashtray into the wall and raise welts until it stops clanging.

The blood on his chest inspires me anew, and I pick out a candle, lighting it silently. Sitting still, I let Mills settle back into a sweaty chest rhythm. The candle hovers above his pinched tit as I move my other hand next to his hood. SNAP! Go my fingers and the first droplets of wax hit the alligator clamp. SNAP! More wax, other tit. Back and forth, fingers snap, wax builds. Mills arches deliciously, as far as his ropes will let him. I walk around him for the remainder of that quarter hour, dripping wax across his chest and stomach to the sounds of heavy boot steps, finger pops and table strikes. For a finale I set my watch down next to his head. I wave the candle flame back and forth below his bare feet until the timer beeps in his ear, at which point I let the flames directly lick at his arches then pull away. Even the gag can't block Mill's screams as they burst from under the hood. I lean in next to his ear and snap my fingers twice, but do nothing. He flinches each time.

"Ah, Ah Ah asshole…time's up," I whisper. I start undoing Mills' blindfold. "It's time to let you see what I'm doing. You just keep on thinking about my partner and your drugs and why you're here. Fifteen minutes from now and I'll take your hood off and the gag out, then you and me can talk some more." For the first time in almost three hours, light gets to Mills eyes. His hooded head waves back and forth like he's trying to dodge their beams. He recovers and stares at me, all uniform and power, and I see his all the way terror. But now there's something else. Anger! That makes me happy, it means there's still something left to break. It makes my dick throb with newfound excitement.

"You didn't get to see me put these on, but you can watch 'em come off. Besides, I want to do it while the gag's still in your mouth. And just because I like you, I want to warn you that this'll hurt very, very much." I let Mills prepare himself for what's coming and I'm treated to seeing him tense up. My gloves roughly grab at his chest and squeeze his pecs as tight as possible. It does hurt, I can hear the scream from inside the hood. "Now be a good little dope dealer and count down with me," I tell him as I position my thumb against each nipple. "Three, two…are you with me, asshole? ONE!" My thumbs pop the alligators right off both nipples at the same time and Mills' gag can't contain the wail that erupts behind it. He gives me the most fucking satisfying scream so far tonight, and for a moment I think he may just pass out. That would've been hot, but he stays awake for me to squeeze more blood from the raw teeth marks on each tit. Candle wax cracks away from where I'd left it pile up.

"You cooled down from the wax, fucker? You want more? Maybe I should let it run someplace new, huh? There's blood on your chest, asshole." I let my voice start escalating again. "Two little blood spots. Just like on my partner, except his spots weren't little like your spots. No, no. And in a couple more minutes I'm gonna open that mouth-hole of yours and you're going to tell me things I don't even want to know." I grip his chest muscles and twist them as far as I can. Mill's wailing is like music. "If not, like I told you, I got enough chain here to sink you so god damn deep that even a dredging operation won't pull you up. So you better tell your new friend everything he needs to hear, or I'm going to take you off of this table and make you think this was just a warm up."

I take my Bowie knife and get it under his belt loop, cold steel slicing the waistline and I savagely slash away at the legs, till there's nothing left but ribbons and jockey shorts. The panic has gone back into Mills' eyes, but I still haven't broken him all the way down. His eyes may have watered; I still haven't taken him to the point where he's crying for me. Begging ain't even good enough. All punks in this officer's private prison cry for the jailer, or they don't go home. I like the screams, but all that's here is a bunch of meat freezers and a parking bay, so he can scream all he fucking wants. Until he cries, it won't get me off.

Fifteen minutes is up. I pop the valve on the gag and listen to the hiss as the air flows out from the bulb. Mills tries to spit it out, but the hood keeps it in place. He's already cursing and yelling, that anger he showed a few minutes ago has welled back strong! Fuck yeah. I can see that I'll have to work harder to make this punk give me what I deserve. Just to piss him off some more, I leave the limp gag bunched up between his gums and I grab his head in both hands. I stand at the head of the table; Mill's wrists still roped in their place and grab his head hard between my gloves.

"Shut up, you worthless fuck!" I let my voice drop back into its most threatening rumble. "So now you're gonna get pissed off at me? "Where the FUCK do you think you are? Who the FUCK is wearing the uniform here? You don't get a fucking quarter. You can't call someone who cares! I don't care! I haven't done half of even what I'd like to do to you, because when I take you to the station with your confession on tape, I don't want you showing any more marks than a couple of bruises! You reading me, asshole? Or is this the way you sounded when you pulled the trigger? No refined, mild mannered rich shit single guy, but noisy fucking dope head with a gun? Is that it?"

I take my uniform's tie from around my neck and loop it around his. Then I pull it tight. "You're still breathin' because I let you breathe." I grab his head again and squeeze it like a walnut. "You're still thinkin' because I haven't crushed your fucking skull...and don't you think I can't. And you still have a dick because if I cut it off now, I can't beat it to shit later. You got that, dick head?" I rip the hood away from his sweaty shiny shaved head and drop him back on the table. His skull hits with a thud and a new cut spurts open. He's back in the panic zone now, pleading with me, but we're too far into this for me to just dump him at his house. Under my uniform, my dick is screaming. I'll get the tears I want, but I may have to get them by splitting Mills' ass in half. I just have to work him up to a point where I know I can get both at once. That means keeping the former Mr. Perfect just scared enough to be thinking I'll go totally crazy and fuck him up good.

For the first time, Mill's shows signs he's cracking. He pleads. Like a sixteen year old getting a traffic ticket with Daddy's car, he pleads. "Sir, what do you want, what do you need?!? I didn't do anything, I don't know you, I don't know who killed your partner, I don't have any drugs, and I can give you money if you just let me go! Nothing else, just let me go! Jesus, man I'll never tell, I swear!"

He's gettin' close. Bet I could make him cry right now if I gave him a dollar amount and agreed to his "terms." But Hell, where's the fun in that shit? I'm the cop here, he's in my workshop and I'll set the rules.

"I don't need your money, asshole. You know what I want? I want my partner back, I want him to walk in that door right now and say, 'hey it's okay, I'm not gone anymore.' But both of us know that's not going to happen. I know what I want, I want your voice on tape, telling me why you killed him and where the crystal is. Then we'll negotiate you a ride home. Meanwhile," I go to my humidor, "I want another cigar. Okay, asshole. When I put my hood over that worthless brain of yours, did you do what I told you? Did you think about how hot this cigar gets when I smoke on it? I sure hope you did, cause now you're gonna find out."

I go over to the rack and get a leg spreader and a solid metal collar. Stretching the bar between his ankles, I cuff his feet into place then untie the ropes. I open up the metal collar and put it around his neck, but pull off my uniform tie and get it back around my shirt. "This baby weighs about twenty pounds, asshole; I want my tie back, but I think I like the sight of something around your neck." Adjusting my tie in the mirror, I return to the wall rack and pick off a pair of solid leather wrist restraints. I padlock them to the collar, then one wrist at a time, untie him from the table and secure each hand by the side of his neck.

"Get up off the table, punk." I push him over the edge and catch him standing. Dragging him over to one of the cell doors, I chain Mills' collar to the bars and clip his legs to eye swivels in the floor. "You may have thought you were singing back there," I told him. "But that ain't the right fucking song." I start rubbing my uniform against his nakedness, giving him a hint of maniacal lust. I take away the shades and stare direct into his eyes. "I got a brand new song for you to learn before all this is done with, asshole. You just remember that." I get a match and let its fire leap to the end of my cigar. The first big plumes go directly into Mills' face, but it's that first eye contact that shows him what's really coming.

He gets to see my eyes and they scare the living hell out of him. Once again, inside, I'm laughing like crazy. Oh yeah! He's mine alright!

Mill's is a few inches shorter than me, so getting close to his face is easy, even with him in a standing position like this. I maneuver behind the steel bars so my hand can still reach around his chest and I can whisper into his ear. I let some lazy smoke drift across his face and then I start playing with his brain again. "Your chest isn't too hairy, punk. But I saw some curly stuff there in the middle." I get the red tip in close and singe baby fuzz. The smell of burning hair gets into his nose and he squirms. "Don't move too much, dickhead. Otherwise, this cigar is going to hit you and that won't be fun. I'll just have to light it again." Mills gets still. "Smart punk, there wasn't much there to lose, so let's have a go at your armpits." I puff a few more times and let the tip graze back and forth under the joint. It makes a great sizzle sound. "Yeah fucker, I like that. Let's make them match." I come round front and heat shave his other pit. I take hold of a few shorthairs and don't say a thing. The response is priceless...Mills gives me an animal, guttural moan. I wordlessly reheat the coal and stroke it up and down the belly, letting the heat tease the muscles in his gut. My gloved hand yanks his dick roughly and the loud singe of pubic hairs makes Mills shudder at the same time he forces him- self to remain stock still. I squeeze the shaft hard and shift it to the other side, clearing away the other side of his nest. A howl emits low in Mills' throat, and I let his cock and balls drop. "What's left, asshole? I got most of your pubes, and since I shaved your head, there's nothing up there...oops hold on...I see something I missed." Stepping back for a couple seconds, I let the ash get hot and red. Taking Mills' head in another elbow lock, I let the tip move dreadful slow at his eye. He really starts to fight me, but I just let my arm squeeze tighter, bringing the cigar where Mills can only stare it down like a big red hot Cyclops. Then I deftly sweep it up, singe his eyebrows and drop my hold just as quick. It's fuck- ing beautiful!

Mills is just hanging there, totally wasted from that last pass. I tilt his head up, cigar back in my mouth. "One other thing, puke. Hair ruins the taste of a good cigar, and my ashtray is all the way over there..." I point at the table..." and I need a place to put this baby out. From where I see it, I got three choices. Your tit, your tongue or...burning end first up your asshole. What do you think?" Mill's gives me nothing in reply. I squeeze his jaw open, and pull his tongue out. "You think you got enough spit in there that it won't burn your buds off?" Mills is frozen solid. I take hold of the cigar and let it smolder near his face. I rub his jockey shorts. "Damn, these are in the way! But I gotta put this out now..." I drive the cigar into a big blob of candle wax. It hangs there, hot in his chest. The punk is still fucking dry eyed! I take off my leather gloves and pick up a different pair from my collection. I let it fly into Mill's face. He screams again.

"Sap gloves asshole! Saps like the ones you get hit with. Two pounds each. Ready?" I pull them on and hammer his pecs. Making dual fists, I just start pounding like he's a door and I'm looking for the owner. "Make 'em tight, fucker, 'cause I'm sick of this shit and I want answers." I slap his face hard enough to hear his jaw pop! "Tighten your stomach, here I come," I start pummeling his gut like it was his chest and I can hear Mills trying to keep up breath wise...and I suddenly realize that I really do have a tough bottom on my hands. I look at his underwear and...fucking A...he's hard! Still scared, but hard. I slide my baton out and wave it in my hand a couple times, then jam it into his gut. He TAKES it. Fuck yeah! I got license now. I start swinging that fucker into his chest, stomach and thighs and all he does is holler...and not a 'stop' in the streak. I finally get so hot that I can't control myself anymore. I drop the baton and swing Mills around so he faces the iron door. Rip strip the briefs away and let him have it. No lube, no prep, nothing. Just my big cop cock up his tight white ass, and his naked sweaty back against the heaving chest of my uniform shirt. My badge digs into his shoulder scraping it raw and I can hear Mill's screaming...but it ain't in pain. He's getting something he's probably been wanting since I got him in here, a hot police fuck. Then suddenly I get what I want. Mill's is sobbing! Fuck YEAH! He's finally come undone and that's exactly what my dick needed to hear. This punk had me hot from the moment I saw him throwing attitude in the bar and I've got him crying! That's when I blast my load like I haven't felt in months, one that will leak out from this punk's ass from now until the middle of next week.

Damn! I gotta prop myself up after that! It leaves me with one last problem. I took Mills all the way down and now I'm left with a thoroughly fucked punk in my private prison who thinks I want him dead. I readjust my uniform and put my shades back on. I go to one of the cells and make sure there's a bed sheet and pillow in place on the cot. I toss a set of coveralls into the cell. I unlock Mills' feet from the spreader bar. I unfasten the collar and undo the wrist restraints. I push him into the cell and watch him collapse on the cot. I slam the cell door shut. I grab a spare cigar and stick it in my shirt pocket. I switch off the light on my way out.

I'll just fucking worry about it tomorrow.

FIRST NIGHT IN THE NEW APARTMENT

It's only a few days after I've moved into the new apartment, a single bedroom bungalow near the 101. Most of the boxes have been unpacked, but there are plenty of belongings merely scattered about. The three most important articles are up and set in place; the stereo, the computer and the bed. An Elvis Costello CD is playing in the background, "Imperial Bedroom," appropriately enough. In my life, it has always been this way; the stereo is always the first thing to get into place!

Next in proper housebreaking manner, I have asked you to come over to visit. Even with the apartment in its extreme disorganized state, our conversations and friendship have intertwined and locked together so firmly that the idea of your being my first guest appeals to me strongly. I do my best to neaten the boxes before your arrival.

When you do appear, it is with an Ace Hardware bag in your hand, which I really don't think much about, after all, it isn't much bigger than a sandwich bag, so where's the fuss in that? I show you the kitchen, bathroom, bedroom and main space; it takes about 60 seconds.

I offer you a place to sit; my second hand sofa and chair are all I have to spare you. My back is turned for just a moment when you make your move. I remember what you say about your strength and agility, for a first time I feel the physicality of it. You have moved in behind me with what was in your Ace hardware bag, a roll of wide silver duct tape. One muscular arm around my chest and the other hand slapping a strip of the tape across my mouth, and you have effectively pushed me into the bedroom and down on the bed.

You quickly pin my wrists behind my back with a few quick

turns of the duct tape, and the same is done to my ankles. I am completely taken by surprise, both by the quickness and the crudeness of it. I'm fully clothed and fully helpless on my bed, you are standing over me with a smile on your face and roll of silver tape in your hand. I fight my restraints, but it's obvious, you got me good!

Your smile doesn't waiver as you add a few more strips of tape to my face, perfecting the gag, then beginning to further assert your control over the situation by adjusting my shirt and pants to a position that suits your desires. My shirt is pulled over my neck and shoulders, left to hang behind me next to where your tape encircles my wrists and lower arms. My belt and button fly get undone and the jeans are yanked down around my ankles. I know you had bondage sex with me in mind long before you arrived, but this show of dominance surprises me. Both, in that with anyone else I'd be struggling madly to escape and in the sense that a sneak attack is something I wouldn't have expected from you.

Helplessness excites you in this case, you have begun removing your clothes. Stripping down to your boots, you light one of your favorite seven inch cigars and begin ritualistically touching me. Your own arousal is plainly evident: all nine inches of you extends away from your powerful physique. I now understand what your plans are, and I grow afraid. It is the ultimate conquest that you have been warning me of. You plan on taking my ass, even if it means taking me in this sordid manner of surrender. I wonder if the idea of rape as submission got you excited enough to try...or if you just knew that if, by pushing the envelope this little bit harder into a forbidden territory and on a new setting, you could get away with it.

All these questions are useless now. I've always known you as a very reasonable man, and again I'll get a taste of how intuitive you really are. I've wanted you to train me to take that massive cock of yours, but have never been able to pass my ego and fear enough to ask you for your help. Now I'll get it, because you've taken your self assuredness and brought it right into my apartment on your first visit. Cigar smoke is beginning to fill the room and will leave its scent after you have left, your pre cum is manifesting at the pierced end of your cock, your powerful hands roughly massage my body and your voice, always reassuring and stable even at its most commanding, is describing how you have every intention of giving me my first fuck in the new apartment.

It is the compactness of the place that adds to the tension. There's not much more here than a functional four walls and they barely contain the ravenous sexual animal inside of you. If this were a zoo cage, you would be pacing in front of the display bars, openly flaunting both your self-confidence with your self aware-ness. I can feel it now; you have taken over the apartment before I've even had a chance to establish the territory as my own. My boxes lay half emptied around the two rooms as your boots side step them.

It is your boot prints that will make their initial impressions on my new living space, not anything I have set up or hung on the walls. It will be the ejaculation from your penis cumming inside me that will scent the mattress for sexual ownership, not my jacked off seed. The apartment closes in around me until there are no longer two rooms, only one. You continue working me, gentle but firm, and even the bedroom shrinks down to just a sphere that encircles you as you move about the bed that I am helplessly bound upon.

There is no escape from our destination. You have made your plans and even if I could (or wanted to?), protest and escape are impossible. Your fingers are teasing my ass now, getting my hole to open and take the lube, a heavily greased dildo is soon being slowly twisted, turned and pumped in place of the fingers. My face and body are sweating...anxiety and anticipation...your words keep me away from falling off into the chasms of panic. You knew all along that I'd take it from you, you keep telling me.

You're right. My ass is relaxing now that you keep me from fear, even though that monster dick will be, without a doubt, the largest object ever admitted into my cavity. I lay on the bed, look-ing like some b-porn movie bondage victim while you take your patience and time to continue your dominance over me. The sound of your words, the touch of your hands, the smoke from your cigar and the assuredness of your presence all contribute to my slow falling away into a deeper submission. I can only describe it as near hypnotic. Even though I couldn't break away physically, mentally the transformation has taken place. You sense this yourself as you push my wrists up a bit for a clearer shot at my submissive ass. You lube yourself up and ever so gently, enter me for the first time.

My ass is splitting in a roar like I'd never dreamed of. My shouts remain behind my duct taped lips...even with your command of the situation; this part still feels like rape! I have nor want any part of this, at the same time my core is begging, whimpering for you to finally, please, give it to me, make yourself complete and finish with your planned conquest. Of course that isn't the point...my surrender is as absolute as you could ever have asked of me. You took control and the slow attack of your cock continues unabated, as do my whimpers and moans as I feel it filling me.

I open my eyes for a second as your motions catch up with the rhythm of your desires, and there is no more "I". Just SIR as you touch the inner switch that makes me SIR's submissive and turns off my ego, just as Sir promised. You make me feel your danger in these close quarters, where the bondage on my body matches the tightness of the room space. A sex animal is being let out into a micro-arena where Sir feels safe, you control me and there is no other place where the beast can run away and commit damage. Sir takes advantage of me this way; it's your privilege. Sir allows me to connect with the sense of dignity that makes your passions hotter, it is obvious with each move of your body, that Sir is enjoying the pure, unsophisticated primal domination the setting allows you. There is unbelievable heat in your presence, and I not only feel the savage sex in each of Sir's thrusts, but your pride in knowing you are able to utilize me in chartering your course to this level of psycho-eroticism.

And as I look on the bed-stand plainly visible next to the hardware bag, there are a series of eye bolts and screw hooks. It looks like the new apartment will be getting a few new furnishings wherever Sir thinks they will do the most good.

BLACK GLOVES, WHITE MAGIC

I look into the face of my lover at the moment I derive the most joy from. Just as he begins to slip into that nether world where total submission is equaled by his own personal satisfaction, there is an aura of bliss that as his Master, only I know how to take him to. He knows that his surrender is my right, yet I am not so vain as to recognize that the balance could only be addressed by the pilot in this journey. When I lay him flat on the bondage board and start twisting the night black plastic wrap around those skin tight rubber pants of his, it's almost like I'm compressing his very soul. His neoprene vest disappears beneath each turn, until I've pushed his essence to the very base of his skull.

At that precise instant, a glow moves into his features that can only be described as an embodiment of his spirit. Lord, the satisfaction that look brings to my heart.

His shoulders were the last thing the stretch film covered. Arms crossed mummy style over his chest give him an ancient, god-like appearance. I bring my face close to his as that aura enters the contours of his face. "I love you, boy," I whisper at that moment.

He sighs deeply, the breath of contentment. "Thank you Sir," he responds back from some other world. I see his shoulders slightly twitch; it's my way of knowing that his enclosure remains a non-hazardous one. Without having to look, I know that his encased cock is stiff and pleasurably sensitive under all his rubber and plastic. He breathes deep from pleasure again, his blindfolded eyes trying to follow where his Master's voice is coming from. "Sir, sometimes I wish that this rubber didn't just stop at the top of my skin. Sometimes I wish it went all the way through me, so I could become the rubber boy you've always thought about."

I pick up a Russian gas mask and begin stretching its skull cap over his head. I allow myself the slightest chuckle as I repeat to him that old cliché "Be careful of what you wish for boy..."

"...because you may just get it."

"Yes, Sir, I know."

I pull the mask over his head and finish totally wrapping my rubber slave's still form on the table. Lighting a Maduro, I lean back in my Master's chair to adore the shining, long black plastic and rubber cocoon just a short distance away. I have planned this night in the playroom to be a special one, an anniversary present of sorts. He has remained my loyal, faithful boy for three years now, learning about rubber as I guided him, scene by scene. As his Master, I filled his desires and dreams even as he gave into my whims and fancies. It was as perfect a union as I had been hoping for all my life. As a gift for him, although dangerous, I will attempt something that will bring both the greatest fulfillment either has ever known.

What he doesn't know about was my apprenticeship, still ongoing as a sorcerer. I've come far these five years, and have been practicing my spells diligently. Tonight is to be the night I will try something very special, yet very risky. The herbs and the chemicals are laid out before me, as are the tools I need to grant my slave his deepest wish. Tonight he will bond with his bindings; he will become the rubber boy from skin to bone.

I start by filling the enema bag with electrolytes and herbs as to spread the potion evenly throughout his body. Then I take the chalks and outline our circle of protection, to hold the malevolent forces at bay. Placing the candles at the four corners of the compass, I light them in their proper order; East, South, West and North. Then, as one last measure of protection, I toss sea salts around the playroom. This is to be a night of white magic, a spell cast for pleasure, not in anger. There is just one, more force left to call on before I can begin, and setting out a pad for them to land on safely, I repeat the chant that will bring a pair of nymphs from the rubber tree spiritual forest into my home.

126

They drop through the portal with a squishy plop, a team of little amber trolls with cheeky expressions and eternally hard dicks. Forget what you've read about hobbits and goblins. Your typical wood nymph is as playful as a child and hornier than a frat house full of pledges. Throughout it all, my slave has remained oblivious in his rubber cocoon, lost inside his own epiphany. He doesn't know that the hands now rubbing at his rubber covered tits belong to eight inch high beings from another dimension. He just feels more pleasure.

The hands never stop groping. "Why do you call on us, Master?"

"My boy has had a wish for a long time," I tell them. "He wants to feel what it would be like to be nothing but rubber flesh on his bones, a living man of black rubber sex."

They continue to roam around my boy, looking like some warped out scene from "Gulliver's Travels." I don't even think they glance up at me while we speak. "That's all? You've made a very simple request," the one closest to me replies. The other is licking at my boy's rubber covered ass cheeks. "We'll help you on one condition."

"What is it?"

Now they do both look at me. "That we can stay and watch."

I consider it for a moment. My slave has no idea that I dabble in the magic arts, and I still don't think I want him to know. "Can you make it so he can't see you?"

"Very simple. Yes!"

"Fine then. Please do stay with us." With that, the two nymphs leap from the bondage table and get into action. They produce a long blanket of rubber to cloak themselves from my boy and a vial that contains a small amount of amber liquid.

"This," they explain to me, "is sap from the eldest tree in our home world. Mix it with the formula in your enema bag, exactly two drops, no more, no less. There is plenty here for later." A small script is then unrolled before me. "Here is the spell you must recite. Say it only once just after you get the sap inside your boy's body and it will infuse his skin with the essence of the rubber plant. He will become rubber, just as you say he wishes."

I look at the words of the spell, it's a brief and basic one. I'm amazed that it's so simplistic. At the same time, I know these nymphs are more than excited by the prospect of a night's worth of voyeurism, so I guess they're anxious for me to get into the scene with a minimal amount of hocus pocus. I open the end of the enema bag and mix in the two drops of sap, as instructed.

"Wait a moment, Master. Not so early." The nymphs take a seat on a cabinet near the bondage table. "Play With him a little; it'll make him excited and more susceptible to the spell."

I strongly suspect that they have more in mind than getting my boy aroused. But they have accommodated me thus far and the last thing I need running amok in my darkroom is a pair of cheesed off nymphs. The enema bag gets hung back on its stand aside my boy and I pick up the medic-scissors from the work tray. The nymphs smile lascivious approval. I take the tips and start cutting through the plastic both along his ass crack and to release his rubber bound cock and balls from their confinement. Then I open the wrappings across his chest and, unzipping his vest, expose his nipples. What was a solid black sarcophagus now shows flashes of pink. My audience leans forward, I swear their drooling is audible.

My boy is still in a state of sensory deprivation. All that has been going on is unknown to him, except for the outer body stimulations he has received at the hands of the nymphs and as the cool rush of air greeted his flesh after my scissors opened up his more sensitive areas, now slick with sweat. Taking my elbow length black rubber gloves, I smear some lube along the fingertips and begin massaging my boy's balls, letting the gel's flow surprise him, and letting my gloved fingers explore down into his ass crack.

Loosened slightly from his bindings, it is still difficult for him to do more than the slightest twists or turns from the probing of my hands. His stiff dick drips shiny pearls of pre-cum onto the black stretch film that remains around his stomach. His inviting nipples fall victim to my slippery fingers, getting even more erect as I pinch and tug at their sensitivity. His arms shudder and shake, bound as they are just below my gloved hands. The breath from within his gas mask hisses out of the breath hole, the only sound he likely can sense under all his coverings. His sexual excitement is escalating, and I pull away from his inviting body to let him cool down. I allow him a few more moments of relaxation before another healthy squirt of lube covers my gloves and the exploration of his ass begins in force.

The nymphs move closer to the table for a better view, but far enough away that they don't interfere. They know that the interactivity between me and my boy is reaching a communal stage and they feed off our energies. My boy's bound hips wave back and forth as my fingers begin their probing, first one, sliding gently in and out, then a second, then third. I know how much he loves the feel of my entire hand against his insides, but not just yet. I merely want enough relaxation around the anus to insert the nozzle.

He is getting close to peaking out, it is time to take my black gloved hands and administer the white magic that I have waited all this time for. I move quickly, sliding the tip of the enema hose in and giving it a moment to settle. His muscles clench around the long gray tube and I release the hose valve. The soft gurgle of fluid begins as the herbs, water and precious sap flows into his intestine. "Recite the spell," the nymphs whisper excitedly, "recite the spell!" I grip the slip of parchment that I was given earlier and repeat the four words thereon deliberately and slowly.

It is then that my boy's rubber glows with a blue-black luster, and the light all seems to draw into the center of the room. I watch the neoprene vest pull itself over my boy's chest and appear to terra form itself to the contours of his body. The nymphs duck behind their rubber blanket as the last sparks of light shoot along his exposed cock and balls, and they suddenly glow blue-black as well.

The whole process takes just a couple of seconds.

"Let him up," the nymphs whisper. "Let us see him!" It takes me a few more seconds to catch my breath, but I pick up the medic-scissors and begin the careful cutting of the stretch film. As I do, I realize that there has been a change in the room; I swear it smells of a just passed electrical storm. My boy's body feels warm as I remove the film, but not damp, the way it usually does after a mummification scene. Most importantly, his skin isn't flesh colored. Just as I was hoping for, it now looks black and spongy. My excitement mounts as I hasten to free the rest of his body from the wrappings, and when I get to the point where I undo his criss-crossed arms, I see his hands. They've become flexible fleshy paws of rubber. And lastly, I look at his dick. It stayed erect throughout and is now a solid mass of hard latex, pulsing like a man's dick should, yet sturdy as the finest dildo. My boy's lungs move smoothly up and down, his gas mask and blindfold still in place.

My audience approves; they applaud and laugh wildly. "As long as he is rubber, his dick will stay that big," the first nymph tells me. The second nymph giggles and adds "And as bonus, he's going to stay horny as a forest beast, too. As long as he stays rubber, he's going to want to be a fuck toy. Just a little something extra you may not have known about, but we didn't think you'd mind. Your boy's wish is now true."

For a fleeting passage, I wonder just what else I might not know about. That thought flashes quickly away. I have given my boy his wish...he has bound with his bindings and as of this moment has become the Rubber-man of the flesh he before merely dreamed of being.

For the first time since my apprenticeship as a sorcerer began, this is my first attempt to cast a spell on a fellow human being. Not just any human, but my one love, the apple of my eye, my boy. After three years together, I decided to give him a gift that he could only receive from his Master. He stands before me and the pair of nymphs he cannot see, a boy of rubber-flesh and mortal bone.

There really was no way to hide what I'd done. Mirrors were an essential part of my dungeon, and all my boy had to do was turn to either side once I'd let him up from the table. He glances from left to right, making sure that his vulcanized features aren't some kind of bizarre trick of the light. Boy's eyes widen, they appear even whiter set back in the blue/black shine of his face. His hair has taken on a new sheen, though it also seems to hold in a set pattern. Every inch of him shimmers like a jewel.

"Happy Anniversary, baby."

He stares at me in disbelief. "What have you done? Sir, Is this what I think it is?" I think he's ready to pinch himself. Almost correct, he takes his rubber hand and strokes his larger than life rubber cock. The nymphs whistle in appreciation. The other hand does pinch himself, tugging at his nipple. "How did you get this rubber to stick on all of me? How come it feels so complete? Is it paint, Sir?"

I note his sexual reaction even through his confusion. The nymphs weren't joking when they said he'd stay horny as a forest creature as long as he was a rubber-boy. Curiously, I wonder if he even realizes what he's doing to himself. The thought excites me. "You always said you wanted to feel how it would be if you were totally rubber skinned instead of just being wrapped up in it. Today, my boy, you got your wish. Thank you for these three wonderful years."

I expected him to come to me then, get on his knees and kiss my feet, the way I've trained him to when he wants to show his deepest gratitude. But he doesn't. In fact, boy doesn't even move. Boy just stands there, that gone look in his eyes, hands playing with his nipple and dick. "Is it a trick, Sir? You're joking with me?" That's when I realize that, as much as he's expressed his desire to possess the rubber body of his dreams, he never realized what the reality would be like...or if he could even achieve it. Now that it was his, he couldn't believe it.

131

"Your Master can do many things you don't know of. That's why all I ask of you is your complete trust. Master needs it from you now. Come to me, boy." Reluctantly, he steps up to me, the smell of his rubber strong. From the table of toys, I lift an exacta knife I keep handy for edge games. "Do you trust me, boy?"

Once more, he hesitates. I take his arm away from his nipple and hold it straight out along my chest. Boy shivers, he doesn't answer my question. Again I notice, his dick remains erect, even in fear. "Answer me boy. Do...you. Trust...me." I press the razor's edge against his forearm.

Boy swallows so hard I feel his body shudder. Or is it just the way the rubber reacts? Even I am getting confused now. "Yes Sir," he replies in a voice so hoarse I barely register the response. I tighten my grip on his arm and ever so slowly, draw a long but shallow cut near his elbow. I take my fingers and pry the edges apart, boy gasps as he sees that no blood flows from the cut, and the area beneath remains black all the way through.

The nymphs go ape. They screech and roll behind their cloak of invisibility, jumping up and down like mad monkeys. "Do him, do him!" they holler. I shoot them a dirty one as I reassure my boy (and myself) that "In your Master's space, many things you never believed possible are. It is still my room, and I can control many situations that you only imagined before. After all this time, boy, your Master can still find little tricks you'll not soon forget." I force my best kindly Master face towards him; right now I'm beginning to remember what the nymphs said about extras I might not have known about. Was boy's fear something they didn't bother warning me of? They were obviously getting their jollies from it, but this was my playroom and I expect things to go as I plan them. Boy has undergone his share of edge games and I have plotted step by step campaigns of terror domination, but always with a set outcome that I'd tested prior to playing the scene out. There had always been a trial run with safety mechanisms in place so that the only danger boy would ever enter was his disobeying me with a loss of nerve. Until, I realized, tonight.

The nymphs are still chanting "do him..." as I realize that I

am being played. Both boy and I are getting our wishes, but so
are they. I make myself remember my teachings about nymphs,
that although they are childish, manipulative and in a continual
state of arousal, they also bore quickly and get irritable. If they
really want to see boy and me getting each others' rocks off, they'll
find a way to do it, pleasantly or unpleasantly.

Boy is still looking at his puncture marks. "Now do you
believe your Master?" He nods, and I feel his confidence return-
ing. I also notice his hand unconsciously shift back to his groin. If
I am to get the most from my boy in his altered state, I am going to
have to push a button guaranteed to hold his attention. But what?
He's totally rubber, so that rules out electricity. How do you shock
an insulator? Hot wax? No... the burns could do permanent damage. Same goes for cigars. It has to be organic and intense. And
the only way I know how to connect with boy at that level is to fist
him. Even as I think the idea through, I can sense the nymphs'
fresh excitement. Once more, I wonder just how much they left
out from the simplicity of this spell.

"Get into the sling, boy," I command him. "For on this night
you'll feel the sense of rubber outside and through you as you feel
your Master entering your insides." This is my playroom. I will
keep control. Inwardly I smile. I am going to be able to play my
boy in a method that he always reacts marvelously to, nymphs be
damned. Boy has already clambered into the sling, setting the
tarry blackness of his heels into the stirrups and grabbing hold of
the back chains. But what to lubricate him with? His ass is
already tempting me, I never dreamed of how amazing a black
puckered rubber rose would look. A quick look at the lube rack
gives me my options, I select an oversize pump bottle filled with
water based gel. I need to keep in mind that any petroleum on my
boy could damage him...I must be extra careful! But right now, the
spell the nymphs gave me to lay on him have made him so horny
that he twitches in the sling, waiting for that first slippery wet latex
covered finger to make its move.

I quickly but carefully load plenty of lube around his hole,
and discover that not only does he instantly relax and open for me,
the blue/black shimmer takes on a new luster as the wetness

spreads. Boy's breath begins it's rhythm, he rocks to and fro in the sling. The black pillar of rubber-cock pulses up and down, and it takes very little coaxing to get the first four fingers inside him. The nymphs leap to the top of the frame, perching above and behind me, now that I'm working boy over they have quieted down. I shape my fingers and thumb into their conical shape as I ease them just ever so close to the outer edge of his ass, then, with a hard pump of lube spurting on top of the glove, I slide the whole glove up to the wrist. Boy takes one sharp breath and moans low as I pause and allow his body to take the invasion. The nymphs let out a low unison whistle. But even as my fingers tickle and tease boy's prostrate gland, I know that this time I'm going to reach for boy's heart...literally.

His rubberized asshole stretches with a delightful easy tight-ness, pleasing my arm as much as my hand is tantalizing boy's inner bulb. I carefully curl my fingers overtop my thumb and let that ball slide back and forth inside my boy, his continued gentle rocking in the sling assures me that he is comfortable with me there. I gently rotate my wrist as he gasps and groans, the spot-light above the sling highlighting the reflective beauty of his rub-ber-flesh body. We continue in this position for just a while longer, then I uncurl my fingers to begin my explorations. A tiny touch here, a slow massage there, my hand creeping deeper inside, my arm growing shorter outside. I encounter a blockage and gently massage it, back and forth, up and down, it relaxes and I continue, measuring progress from the outside, arm hair by arm hair as I disappear into boy's most private place. Then, I feel my goal...his pulse, there, the rush of blood against my hand. Knowing that as many times as my boy may have been touched, here was a place that I alone could feel. And for just this once, in a manner that I can never duplicate again. Boy can feel it, too. I sense the heart-beat of my lover's body coursing around my limb as he reacts to the fullness pounding within him. Again, the white magic of this special evening prevails and the glow enters his features for a sec-ond time tonight. Boy is enhanced by the rubber in his face, it absolutely lights up with pleasure. I grant myself a Master's privi-lege, from my position against his body, I allow myself licks and kisses along his lifted rubber-flesh thighs, my tongue tasting the rubber calves and watching him shiver with the sensations in and out of his body. Now the careful withdrawal, marking progress in the same slow manner, the slippery noises as my arm begins to come away.

There's applause behind me and the reverence is broken. Damn those nymphs...I'd forgotten about my miniature peanut gallery. At the same time, I recognize that they must have been enthralled by the display of unity between me and my lover. True to form, though, they had seen their fill and were getting anxious to return to their ancient rubber forest. They climb back to the center of the bondage table where boy began his evening's odyssey, preparing to leave. I no longer feel the anxiety I had just a few hours before. They begin their own ritual and start calling to their home world. Even though it means causing boy confusion, I call to them, after all, there is one detail left before the night is over.

"How do I bring my boy back to human form?"

They look at me like I've lost a nut somewhere. So does boy. "You mean you want him flesh again after you've brought him to this?" they ask. I nod yes. They pass a look between them- selves and another grin that chills my stomach. Once more, I recall the comment about little things I might not know about. "You can have him back very easily. But why would you want to? Look how hard he is! Keep your boy as rubber-flesh and he will never stop wanting you, nor will he ever want to stop." I do not answer them, partly because I don't want to be drawn into a pitfall, also because I don't want boy to hear me talking to an empty space.

They continue their wait, but their impatience gets the better of them. "Oh bother. It's a very simple thing to annul this kind of spell. Merely reverse the sequence of events and you'll find him to be as bad as new." The one nymph grunts sardonically. "We gave you an improved model. What more could you want? Just turn everything around and you'll get everything you want." Before I can ask how you fist fuck someone in reverse, they throw their cloak into the air and ride it straight up...and out of my playroom.

I curse my foolishness, because the little buggers knew

exactly what they were doing. The longer and more intensely I played with boy, the more complicated it would be for me to undo my efforts. Foolishly, in my desire to give my boy his deepest wish, I had entered into a situation that now had exceeded my training. There was only one thing I could do, embarrassing as it would be. I tell boy to relax back into the sling and I'll go out to the kitchen for drinks. I exit the playroom, head straight for the kitchen phone and, late as it is, call my mentor, Gold.

"Master, I humble myself...I have entered into a situation that I don't know how to get out of." After an apology for waking him at this hour, I begin a brief explanation of the events of my anniversary celebration as he grunted, chuckled, and listened in silence. Sweat was starting to gather on my forehead when he asks me how much I cared about my boy.

"Sir, you must know...after listening to what we've done this night, more than anything else I've encountered in this world."

"There's no need to be scared, student," he reassures me. "The nymphs just figured you knew what you needed to know, despite how tricky they seem to be." I breathe a sigh of relief. It's short-lived, however, as Mentor Gold continued with his instructions. "You won't have to reverse the sequence of everything you've done, just one very important aspect of you and boy's relationship. In order to get back the thing you love the most, you will have to become that which you least want to be..."

This anniversary celebration with my boy has become one of the oddest nights of my life. The nymphs of the ancient rubber forest gave me the ability to turn boy into rubber flesh, but they figured that if I knew how to bring them to my world and help me conjure, I was an experienced enough sorcerer to bring him back without annoying them with sticking around after the show was over. And what a show...the deepest, most movingly spiritual fisting we've ever shared! Yet here I am, shaking in the refrigerator lit kitchen as my sling reclining rubberized boy relaxes in the afterglow. At the other end of my telephone is my teacher, Mentor Gold, as he explains to me the breadth of what I must do to bring my lover back to human form...

"As intense as your session was, did boy ever cum?" No, he hadn't. "Then that's one thing you have to take care of. The nymphs left you some more of the sap, didn't they." I answer yes. "In your drink, drop two drops, but only for your drink and don't let boy take from your drink. And you penetrated him, you topped him, correct?" Again, yes. "Then he must Top you, and he must decide how...without your doing anything more than coaxing him. He must decide the 'how' and you absolutely can not resist his wishes." I protest vaguely, after all, he is my boy, and I control my playroom. "No!" Mentor Gold stopped me sternly. "Remember what I told? You must become that which you least want to be if you want to get back the thing you care for the most. You played right into the mischief of the nymphs, and now, if you want to get boy back...you're going to have to bottom for him."

I swear I can hear the nymphs laughing now, somewhere where I can't see them.

"Just make sure you do it inside the circle of protection, and that there is a soft place for boy to land." I give Mentor Gold my assurances that it will all be there as he instructed, and that I must get back to boy before he becomes suspicious. I also tell him how grateful I am for assisting me at this awkward time and late hour, and that I'll explain everything at length during our next session. "Oh, don't worry," he answers. "Next time you come to me, you'll have plenty to answer for." Mentor Gold chuckles in a manner that makes me wonder just what he has in mind by that remark...and I'm not to sure I really wanted to know. I hang my end of the telephone in its cradle, grab two cold cans for the playroom and return to my boy.

Boy smiles at me dreamily as I hand him his soda. "Even with everything we've done this evening, Sir, I feel like I could just keep going." His hand lazily slides along the length of his ever hard black rubber dick. I take my first step towards bringing this evening back to reality. Since boy's eyes are in a reclining, unfocused phase, I take the tiny bottle of sap the nymphs brought to my playroom and mix two drops into my drink can. Just to make sure that there won't be any problems later, I chug the remaining 16 ounces down in one rush. "You sure were thirsty, weren't you

Sir," boy observes.

"That much action always makes me thirsty." I look at my boy again, trying to keep from acting forced. "You get one more gift tonight, boy. For every tease, torment or tie-down that you've ever experienced, here's your chance to get your Master back." Boy opens his eyes wide; there is a mischief there that I've never seen before. I help him out of the sling and lead him to the bondage table, the circle of protection still visible to me on the platform around it. His hands glow with that rubber beauty, as he lays them across my shoulders. Now, instead of pulling at his own nipples, he starts twirling his spongy digits against mine. I look into boy's face and a scary recognition becomes apparent to me. His eyes and smile are more than a bit, but not quite exactly like that of the nymphs. I blink and the face of my boy returns. It's a fearful second, and I place fresh candles at their proper directional points as boy continues asking hesitant but aroused questions.

"You don't need my permission, boy. This is a moment for you to take control of the playroom, a moment when everything you've learned grants you a session of unconditional surrender from me," I answer. Boy selects a pair of wrist and ankle rubber restraints from the rack and while he does, I re-spread sea salts around the table. He takes a coil of rope, I reposition a wrestling mat near the bondage board. He chooses a tape for the stereo system; I light the candles in the reversed order north, west, south, and east. Each time he concentrates on gathering tools for his opportunity with me, I hastily reestablish the inviolability of the white magic's order. At only one time do I stop boy from his selections, and that is when he lifts a ball gag from the wall rack. "I'm sorry boy," I tell him. "There is just one option that I do have to allow myself, and that's the ability to speak. I hope you understand." He looks at me strangely, but the moment passes. I am beginning to feel a strange rumbling in my stomach that I recognize as the takings of the rubber sap infiltrating my system. It's my signal to begin now.

With the four candles casting flickering shadows across the table, boy takes my hand from his rubber flesh and positions me face down on the table. His body glows like Saint Elmo's fire as he tightens the rubber restraints around my wrists and then ties them off to the head of the board. Each ankle gets a separate rubber cuff and then a corner of the table, boy spreads me so securely that I forget just how out of form my body has become...even while demanding that he maintain a firm body for my pleasure. Straps at my thighs expose my ass. What ever plans my Rubber-boy has for me now, he's obviously been thinking about them for some time.

I feel the cool soft slickness of his rubber as he draws his hands along the length of my restrained body. He lifts my head back so that I can see myself in the mirror; I stare at myself over my rubber-cuffed wrists. His black, tight and lustrous body stands shining in the mirror alongside my helpless form, and I realize the nervousness and helplessness that it brings to me. For the first time ever in my own playroom, I am about to sacrifice control. Even sharper is the knowledge that, by relinquishing my command of the situation, I have placed us both in terrible jeopardy. If boy decides to change the order of the situation, an irreversible disaster could result. Yet as I look at boy's reflection in the mirror next to my prone position, I still feel the love for him that only a Master can possess, the most seductive of emotions. Boy feels my tension and misinterprets it, even while picking up a wrap-around rubber blindfold. He brings his head next to mine as he de-sights me, whispering an unexpected reassurance.

"Trust me as you would trust yourself."

The blindfold slips over my eyes and I feel him moving away from me...then a cool stroking from my neck to the small of my back. Recognizing it as he repeats the gesture, I brace myself for what I know is about to come. When the first light kiss of the rubber-cat flies across my shoulders I start with the breathing exercises I've tried to teach all beginners that have ever been bound to my cross. A gentle warmth creeps into my blades, I know that they must be taking on a redness as boy increases the force and speed of the rubber-cat's swings. I wince and hold my tongue, both out of pride and fear that crying out might tempt boy to use the forbidden gag. The power of the flogging continues to grow as boy shifts the blows from not only my back, but to my vulnerable ass as well. I recall my lessons in concentration, telling myself to spread the pain across the body and allow the good sensations to replace them. Still, boy has taken three years' worth of my pleasures and learned well from them. He attacks sensitive areas to surprise me and maintains the ebb and flow of pain as my tolerance builds, my brain shrieks but I allow my mouth no more than the barks and grunts each blow forces through my throat. To help defer the growing agony of my boy's torment, I recall how the light seemed to suck into the center of the table when the original spell took its effect. The heat in my body mounts, boy has switched from the lashes of the rubber-cat to the solidity of the rubber pledge paddle. Boy concentrates entirely on my ass and thighs as the pain gives way entirely to the burning pulses of blood heat.

I'm now alert to a new sensorial connection. My nostrils fill with the scent of hot rubber and I immediately link it to boy. Through all his exertions, the rubber-flesh that's covering him is heating to the point that his skin is giving off the strong scent of pure rubber! As the rhythm of his blows continues unabated against my ass and the rubber sap infiltrates my body, it is that one last piece of the puzzle that connects it all. The sensations break from fire throbbing to pleasure as my muscles release their endorphins. The tension melts and my body relaxes, and bless boy for being such a rapt pupil, he recognizes it for what it is. His beatings stop right there as his rubber fingers stroke my shoulders, their Vulcan cool contrasting to the inferno of heat that lingers just below the surface of my skin. I'd forgotten what has led to this reversal of roles as his hands continue stroking, working their way lower and lower down my pleasure/pain filled body. Somewhere in my bound struggles, I've unwarily become rock hard, my dick twisted up and stiff under my stomach. That's when I realize what boy has in store for me next.

The bondage table shudders just a little as he climbs on top and between my forcibly immobilized legs, the heat of his rubber body giving me an almost radar-like ability to judge his motions. Boy's rubberized hands move to separate my cheeks and I feel the sudden cold massage of lube against my asshole. I know what's coming. And as many times as I have claimed that I am Top only, I resist the urge to cry stop and give in to the submission that I must in order to bring the evening to a close. I remember what mentor Gold said about boy having to cum while topping me, and that I can't alter his decisions if I want him back the way he started. His fingers are probing me now, first the middle one, then two, and three, pushing and thrusting, lubing me up completely. I fight the impulse to scream and remember what boy said as he lowered the rubber blindfold over my eyes.

"Trust me as you would trust yourself."

I remember those words as the tip of his hard rubber dick penetrates my hole and the heavy application of lube makes it glide like a slick sausage. And I remember the last thing I have to do as the searing stretch turns to the ecstasy of prostate massage. For the love of my boy, I begin to whisper "Soreb crib ebust burleber." His momentum and fury increase, so does the frequency of my intonation. Boy is shouting so loud in his ride that my mumbling couldn't possibly be anything he'd hear. "Soreb crib ebust burleber, soreb crib ebust berleber..." The noise in the playroom is reaching a deafening point, I remain trapped beneath the mad thrusts of my boy and the scent of his rubber body, my muscles tight against their bindings and my body rocking against his out of control lusts. I can't believe boy could get any louder, but he does so, in a fury I never knew him capable of. Then the thrusts stop and shudders begin as he explodes deep within me, his hot seed pouring into me like lava and I feel the chemical reaction with my tiny intake of sap...my balls burst with the pent up cream of the mysteries of this night. Even with the blindfold still depriving me of my sight, I see light flowering in the back of my brain, cascading from front to back under my eyelids and I feel boy as he springs off me. No, make that as his body blasts away from mine like an ejection seat. Mentor Gold's warning about a soft pad to land on...was that where boy is? I can't see, can't move, can barely hear, and can only wait...

...until I feel a pair of hands wrapping themselves around my head. A low, low voice in my ear, my boy as he whispers "It's done, Sir." His hands release me, thighs first, then ankles and wrists. "Close your eyes, Sir." Boy lifts the blindfold up and off my head and I see him again. Only this time, colored by the beautiful tones of skin I first fell in love with in the smoky air of a bar patio. Boy helps me to my feet, my ass burning and throbbing, his eyes filled with the understanding of what it takes to be a true Master.

"Happy anniversary, boy," I tell him for the second time this evening. My body is feeling a touch wobbly as boy kneels before me, the strong scent of rubber still surrounding him as his back arcs down and pauses while kissing each foot, just as I taught him three years ago.

There is a certain amount of magic inherent in all relation- ships; boy and I both recognize that fact. I now know that every time I start a session by slipping a black gloved thumb deep into boy's mouth, his love and understanding of rubber grows, too. As for that one night in my playroom, there will always be a tiny piece of white magic where both of us had a wish come true and our knowledge of each other took a mystic leap.

SOMEDAY NEVER COMES

The white room, it's better than the black room and I love it when Master takes me there. All else falls away and although I hate to sound selfish, sometimes it's hard to even remember that Master is the one guiding me. I simply know He loves it as I do when he brings me here. His best toys may be in the dungeon, but our most special moments are when he gets his boy in the white room, a chamber so thoroughly different than the black room. Our trips within are usually His shortest...yet at the same time, my longest.

There is no now, then or later. Only here, I hesitate to date these trips, I can only call them "some days."

Master has me here now and we share the moment as he whips me to blood, the last protective layer of humanity removed as I hang from his cross. Knuckles going white as I grip the chains; He has carried me over the threshold and we know that, from this point, there is no turning back. I take a deep breath and it catches in my abdomen, seeping from my chest to the erogenous zones below.

I open my mouth to cry out, yet there is no sound. My mouth tastes the air; the oxygen tastes cold, like spring water. My nose and throat take their fill of it, my body is immersed. I feel like I am swimming in it, not merely floating but swimming. As if the slightest push would lift me from this ocean and send me soaring from a pool of air and into the oceans of light surrounding me. My Master's palm melds to my chest and his strength lifts me. With smooth suddenness, I rise swanlike, arms outstretched and mouth open, lifted up to enter the light of the white room.

Master must be also sharing these feelings too. There's no

possibility a single engine could supply the drive that these reveal-ings consist of. We are together like two silver salmon in perfect water. For the first time, able to close their eyes from the light of a world they've never been able to avoid staring at, for the first time able to experience their world from within, from behind the dark-ness. The water turns turbulent, winding upwards, away to some-thing stronger and bolder than a world below the surface. Do fish become dispirited once they discover no way to ever comprehend what is above the world of the water?   When do they give up try-ing to determine what is just beyond reach of their particular uni-verse? Master knows how to break the water and I slip a dimen-sion above it. He allows me this in his white room.

It is not a birthing; that is too simple a word to describe it. Like a bulb to the flower that peels back husk before exploding to the surface, maybe that is more accurate. Yet at the same time, the husk never stops scaling back, it sheds away and my skin becomes awash with what is in myself, warm and sexually scent-ed, tangy and metallic, my own body bathing itself in this space. My body moves not as an infant's. How could a man foal, from a tiny knock kneed pony to a stallion before he shakes his mane to the sky in mere seconds? That is what it feels akin to. Yet not quite, because there is no formal way to elucidate what my soul feels during this trans-version.

Have I cum, yet? In this room, the thought does not cross your mind. But the roiling of water and rush of twin bodies has gone beyond warmth to friction, to combustion, fusion and very soon, the throes of release. I hear a voice now, not my Master's, not mine, but a merged harmonious musing of both, a chorus from a single being.

"Have you cum yet?"

"No Sir"

"There is no someday for a slave as good as you, only the present. Return, boy!"

That last breath taken gushes out and there is another

sound, the victorious scream of submission in toto, my legs turn gelatinous and I begin sliding to the floor. My whole body is quivering. I feel the rush in my stomach and the hot throbs as my entire body explodes in teeth coloring mind flashes. The concrete underneath me is channeling power from the earth up and into my entirety as semen tears cock, the almost electric pulse into my restraints, of soul funneled into guts then out through the penis slit. I breathe again, a full breath rushing to my lungs once more.

"Good God Boy, are you there?" whispers Master. A voice I'd never heard him use before.

"Yes Sir." I whimper.

I notice that Master has cut me down from the cross and has a vial of salts in his hand. There is blood on his arms, I recognize it as mine. It is His now, He has taken it from me just as much as I have earned the privilege of losing it.

He smiles and beneath the sweat, blood, and exertion, we share a singular secret. Entry is for the chosen few to the white room, and it only occurs on a special "someday" when neither of us expects it to. For this, Master and I are blessed. For many others, someday never comes.

TIM BROUGH

Tim Brough was born in May 1960 and grew up in Central Pennsylvania eating Hershey candy and Lebanon Bologna. He became a bookworm and lost all his body hair by the time he was seven-the condition is known as Alopecia. By the seventies, in addition to being the family bookworm, he started discovering he was a rock and roll freak.

Tim discovered that not only did he enjoy writing, he had a genuine flair for it. After graduating from Palmyra High School in 1978, he was off to Susquehanna University where along with his studies he found himself doing stand-up comedy, singing in a punk band and even dressing up as a clown for a summer at Hershey Park.

Even though Tim has laid down roots in seven states, he currently calls Philadelphia home. He is currently working on a second collection of stories from his previous writing venues and working on several novels.